DEDICATION

For my daughters. I love you so much. Stay weird.

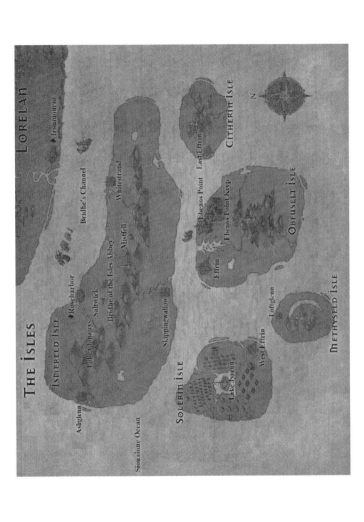

THE ISLES

LORELAN

ISHEFELD ISLE

Ironbourne

Roseharbor

Bridhe's Channel

Ashglenn

Lake Unuorn

Saltwick

Bridhe of the Isles Abbey

Misfell

Whitestrand

Flappingwallow

Stonaline Ocean

CITHERIM ISLE

Buenos Point

Last Effrim

Thebus Point Keep

OBFUSELT ISLE

Effrin

SOLERIM ISLE

Lake Sateen

West Effrin

Lofteloun

DETHYSELD ISLE

N

TABLE OF CONTENTS

CHAPTER 1

“ “I’m going to fall through the ceiling and plummet to my death,” Natalie hissed. On her belly and plastered to the roof of the glass garden next to Roseharbor Palace, she pulled herself by the elbows inch by inch across the delicate surface.

“You won’t fall. And cover your damn red hair. Seriously, why did you dye it that color? Someone is going to see us from a mile away.”

Well, at least Natalie could rely on Anli to break the tension. She and her friends had to go undercover to avoid identification by the spies crawling all over Roseharbor city. Despite the inconvenience of dyeing her hair, she rather liked her fiery locks.

However, trespassing on palace property warranted caution. Pulling her hood close to her face, she continued her slow crawl over the roof. Jules, Onlo and Em foll__ behind.

It had been two months sin__ throne room when Jules h

responsible for so much evil.

Unfortunately, Aldworth had turned out to be a puppet for a woman named Ystrelle: Head Councilwoman of Council of Master Gardeners, Secret Keeper for the Isle of Solerin, and psychopath.

At the end of the battle, Jules had hurled a powerful ball of mage energy in an attempt to kill Ystrelle. Their friend and queen, Charlotte, accidentally got in the way. The bolt knocked Charlotte, Ystrelle and all her guards unconscious. Jules, Onlo and Anli had no time to retrieve Charlotte from under the guards; they had picked up Natalie's comatose body and fled.

During Natalie's lengthy recovery from the fight, planning to rescue Charlotte began.

At long last, a tip from a member of the Queensguard Onlo had bribed led them to the top of this glass-enclosed rose garden. The delicate scent of the flowers tempted Natalie to look down, but she had to focus on the Princess.

Please let her be all right, please let her be alive, I hope Ystrelle didn't—

Natalie's precarious grip on the glass gave way and she slid, heart in her throat, expecting her next stop to be in the carefully manicured shrubs on the side of the greenhouse. Pain lanced through her abdomen and back when she hit the end of the rope that tied her to the rest of her friends.

"Ow! Goddess' teeth."

"Better that than falling your death," a deep voice said in the darkness.

Natalie winced. "Yes, Onlo, thank you."

Twisting and stretching her fingers and toes, she found purchase on the slippery surface once more. Upon returning to her original position, she could see the window the guard told them about. She prayed to the Goddess he hadn't lied; that on the other side of those iron bars and panes of glass was the chamber in which Ystrelle kept Queen Charlotte.

crept ever closer, completely certain her own death By some miracle she was able to get close to the window.

One by one her friends joined her. The sight of Onlo still gave her a start; he had painstakingly undone his thick cords of hair. In their place were long, thin braids swept up into a pony tail on top of his head. He wore dark green leathers instead of the black ones he'd earned as someone Attuned to Obfuselt Isles' obsidian megalith. His two deadly daggers loomed ominously over his shoulders ready for him to draw at any moment.

Jules showed up next to Onlo. He'd trimmed his hair extraordinarily short and kept the beard he grew while helping her recover from the battle in the throne room two months ago. In place of his usual fine tailored clothing and the emerald cloak that he, like her, wore as a testament to their Attunement to Ismereld's emerald megalith, he wore a black shirt and trews.

Finally, her best friend Em crawled nimbly alongside Jules. Em now wore a black scirpa, the cloth covering her hair, knotted at the nape and draping down her back. Em had also donned dark pants and a loose-fitting dark shirt that covered the jagged pink scar on her lower left arm—a souvenir of the shipwreck they'd all been in last summer.

"Let's get close to the window," Onlo whispered. "One at a time; I suggest Anli go first."

Anli crept over, grasped the window sill with her fingers and peered above. Natalie watched, her heart beat echoing in her ears. The ever lengthening silence only terrified her more.

Anli slunk back and they all bent their heads to hers. "She's there."

"But?" Natalie demanded, the tone of Anli's voice making the hair on the nape of Natalie's neck stand up.

"Charlotte seems unharmed; I can't see any damage to her," Anli hedged.

Onlo put his hand on Anli's. "Then wh— you so frightened?"

"It's like Charlotte the

been physically harming her, I can't see it. But I think she's broken somehow."

Onlo clenched his fists. "Physically harming someone isn't the only way to torture them. I need to see."

Dread slithered in Natalie's stomach. She'd witnessed Onlo and Charlotte embracing last summer on Obfuselt. The relationship between them seemed to go beyond love in ways she couldn't even describe. If Onlo saw something terrible, she feared what it might do to him.

He returned a few minutes later, hands shaking and a muscle bulging in his jaw. "Anli's right. Something's happened to her mind. We've got to get her out. How can we get through those bars? Ideas. Now."

"You there. What are you doing?" The question echoed throughout the palace grounds. In their preoccupation with Charlotte's condition they'd gotten sloppy. The Queensguard patrol near the garden had spotted them. *Hell in a kettle, Goddess forbid if Charlotte pays for our mistake.*

"Run," Anli said unnecessarily.

Her command was easier said than done. Natalie clawed her way toward the apex, slipping and sliding with everyone else. The rope connecting them all dug into her stomach. Natalie tried her best to keep up as her friends pulled her along.

Reaching the top of the roof she swung her leg over, glass cracking beneath her food as it landed on the other side. Raised voices sounded in the distance. *More guards. Please don't let the glass give way now.*

They slid more than climbed down the other side. One by one they clambered down the ladder they'd left in the shadows. The Queensguard swarmed around the greenhouse, spotting them as Natalie's feet touched blissfully solid ground. They sprinted for their horses. Anli and Onlo leaped on with ease. Jules mounted up in one deft motion while Natalie stopped to give Em a leg up.

"Nat, you know I love Charlotte but I'm a midwife ↑ a spy."

"I know sweeting," Natalie ran for her own horse swung up into the saddle and galloped after her friends. She ventured a glance behind them, hair whipping in her face. *Dammit, they're right on top of us.*

"Faster, love, faster" she urged her horse. Her heart was always in her throat during spy missions but this time it seemed to take a permanent residence, pounding a crazy rhythm that matched her horse's madcap race through the back streets and alleys of Roseharbor. She grabbed a handful of mane and held on for dear life, following Onlo, Anli and Jules, chancing occasional glances to be sure Em was all right.

All they had to do was make it to Jules's house. Jules led the way as he was most familiar with the way out of the city to the outskirts where his family lived.

Her horse skidded to a halt; Natalie found herself slung forward with an unwanted close-up view of Roseharbor's cobblestone streets. Reins dangling and one leg hanging over the saddle, she pushed herself backwards off the horse's shoulder and into the saddle as Jules let out a stream of curses.

A dead-end.

"Dammit, I went the wrong way."

As one, they turned around, the palace guards slowing to a stop and grinning with victory having cornered their prey.

Onlo drew his daggers, deadly sparks of moonlight glinting off the Obfuseltan steel. "Then we will fight our way out."

Natalie threw her leg over her horse's withers and handed her horse to Em. She, Jules, Onlo and Anli formed a wall in front of Em and their mounts. She drew her short staff and counted ten palace guards. Four versus ten.

This is it. My first fight since the battle in the palace throne room two months ago.

Earlier that spring, while fighting a deadly epidemic, she and Jules discovered they could combine their Healing energies to help Heal people. That summer they also learned that Natalie's energy could amplify Jules's electrical mage bolts.

Two months ago, they'd set out to remove the corrupt monarchy from power and find Healer Aldworth, the man responsible for capturing and torturing Jules—twice. She and Jules found themselves captive and outnumbered. Natalie had to donate her energy to Jules so he could blast a way out of the Roseharbor Palace throne room.

The mage bolt that ended the fight almost killed her. She had spent three weeks in a coma and every day since recovering.

Or trying to. She still had daily issues with speaking correctly, bone-draining fatigue and head-splitting migraines each week.

She had no idea how well she could fight today. But the adrenaline burning through her blood gave her hope.

Anli drew her own daggers, the moonlight glinting off of her dark indigo, chin length hair. Jules dropped his hand, palm forward, to his side, the crackling ball of blue mage energy illuminating their foes. Natalie dug her finger nails into her staff.

The guards attacked as one; Natalie picked her opponent, a tall woman with a long brown braid trailing down her back, brown skin, muscles bulging as she swung her battle ax. Deflecting the first crushing blow, Natalie breathed deeply, and let her instincts take over. Eyes on her foe she twisted and turned, whirling and parrying, dodging and kicking and praying that Onlo's training would be enough.

Natalie heard grunts and cries and it took a moment to realize that they were her own. Her anger at Charlotte's imprisonment came out with every blow to her Queensguard opponent. One final strike to the head finished the fight.

Balancing on the balls of her feet, she looked for another person to attack. Anli and Onlo had taken down four people and Jules two. Together, they took down the remaining guards.

Panting, Natalie stowed her staff in its holster on her back. "That was close, too close. We got lop—sl—sloppy." She cringed as she heard herself fail to say the word properly. *Will my brain ever get better?*

"We did," Jules said. "It's my fault about getting stuck in a dead-end, I—"

Onlo held up a hand. "It happened. It's time to move forward now." His dark eyes landed on Natalie and she couldn't quite fathom his expression. "Time to get to our safe house. Is anyone injured?"

Everyone shook their heads rolling their shoulders a bit and shaking off some bruises. They urged their horses through a maze of shadowy, twisted alleys and roads to the outskirts of Roseharbor city.

Natalie heaved out a sigh, the clip clop of the horses' hooves echoing along the meticulously trimmed hedges, wrought-iron gates and giant houses of the neighborhood through which they rode.

They were near their safe house—such as it was. Dread slithered in her stomach and Natalie almost turned her horse around. She'd much rather fight the Queensguard again instead of facing Jules's mother.

CHAPTER 2

"Natalie, for the last time, we're not being followed. And Anli and Onlo checked for people watching the house. Come on."

Natalie glanced at the road and then trudged behind her friends into through the servant's entrance into Rayvenwood House.

They'd groomed and fed the horses, now contentedly munching hay in the stables. All their tasks done; the coast was clear. There was nothing for it but to go inside.

Despite her dread about facing Jules's mother once more, going from the crisp fall night into the warm kitchen was a blessing. Natalie's dog, a large retriever cross named Jake, greeted everyone with a thorough inspection, wet kisses and bruises on their legs from his wagging tail.

The Rayvenwood's cook brought out warm cider and everyone wrapped their fingers around the delicate ceramic mugs, sipping carefully so as not to burn their tongues. Natalie closed her eyes as she swallowed the tart, hot liquid and suppressed a moan of contentment as the warmth spread to her stomach.

McGraw, the family butler and Jules's one loyal companion in the household entered. "Anything I can get for any of you?"

"No, McGraw thank you."

Thank Goddess we have allies in this horrid place. Cook brought out some cold meat, a small wheel of cheese and some leftovers from the morning's breakfast. Bellies full and fingers tingling as the feeling returned to them, they traded ideas on how they could get Charlotte out from behind the iron bars covering her window.

A cold voice came from the stairs. "So you are still up to this silly 'spy' business."

The servants in the kitchen rose to a standing position. A tall, willowy woman with silver-white hair in a perfect chignon stood at the base of the stairs one papery hand on the railing. She wore an elegantly tailored navy blue dress in what Natalie guessed was the latest fashion. Diamonds dripped like icicles from her ears, neck and wrists.

Natalie grit her teeth and stared daggers at her.

Jules gave a small wave. "Hello, Mother," he deadpanned.

"When are you really going to tell me what you are doing here Jules? I grow tired of hosting you and your … friends. It's lucky your father is out of town. By now he would have you married to Queen Charlotte—or thrown you out of the house."

"Mother, as I've explained to you many times: two months ago, Healer Aldworth killed Charlotte's parents. Charlotte herself is now a puppet of Ystrelle, Head Councilwoman of the Council of Master Gardeners from Solerin. She's planning to take over the Isles *and* she's an unbalanced, mentally ill woman. For Goddess's sake, Mother, we must get Charlotte away."

"*Queen* Charlotte, Juliers. And it is you who suffer from delusions. I *will* see you on that throne. You *will* accept Queen Charlotte's wedding engagement and your friends must leave within twenty-four hours." She turned and ascended the stairs with a regal air.

"Why doesn't *she* marry Charlotte and be done with it?" Natalie muttered when she was out of earshot.

Jules snorted into his cider but Em scolded, "Natalie."

But Natalie had had it up to her back teeth with Victoria Rayvenwood. In the month they had been staying in the grand house, she'd witnessed Victoria's disregard for her son, her bare tolerance of Anli and Onlo and her pure hatred of Em—Natalie suspected because of Em's religion.

Victoria, normally a very calm, collected, well-spoken woman absolutely exploded when she found out about Jules and Natalie's romantic relationship. The tirade about Natalie's low birth and being a farmer's daughter from Mistfell went on for an hour.

And much as I hate crawling over glass roofs, any excuse to get out of this wretched house and away from that horrible woman is a welcome one. I wish it was safe to go home. To the Abbey.

Onlo set his mug on the table. "With Mrs. Rayvenwood's pronouncement, it seems we have one day left here; that means we need to find another safe house. And I need to know the fastest way get Charlotte out from behind the iron bars."

"Well, explosives would work but they would draw a bit of attention," Anli said.

"No explosives," Onlo said in a low voice. "But the thought is tempting. Blowing something up would be very satisfying right now."

Natalie nodded blearily at her cup of cider. The fatigue that hounded her every day rolled in like a storm off the sea now that the danger had passed.

"I don't know of any other safe houses in Roseharbor," Jules said.

Natalie glanced at Jules, his left forearm resting on the table, the fingers from his remaining hand restlessly tapping a staccato rhythm on the smooth surface.

A memory flitted across her brain from last spring when

they arrived in Roseharbor trying to treat the epidemic and she suggested they stay at his house. He vehemently shot down the idea. Every day she understood why.

From their whispered conversations at night she knew the burden of keeping their group safe weighed on him. Unfortunately, they had yet to come up with something better.

"So it's agreed then. We return to the palace tomorrow morning."

Natalie tried to blink away the fog in her brain. *Wait, they want to try tonight's plan again. In the* daylight?

"Onlo, we had a hard enough time getting up on top of that greenhouse at night and even then we got caught by the Queensguard. How is one person to get up there during the day without being spotted?"

Onlo grinned and interlaced his fingers. "I have an idea."

CHAPTER 3

Traces of sunlight barely streaked the horizon as Natalie crept across the roof of the greenhouse once again. It was just she and Anli this time. Jules and Onlo skulked in the shrubbery around the great glass structure keeping the route back to Em and the horses clear.

"We're going to fall through this roof I just know it. We left cracks in it last night," Natalie muttered.

Anli nimbly climbed the glass panes ahead of her. "Oh, shut up and stop complaining. All you have to do is look for the cracks so you can avoid them."

"I can't look for them; I can't see."

"You are the worst spy."

"Yes. It's why I became a Healer, Miss Spy."

Natalie and Anli had the dubious honor of returning to the roof this morning. Someone knowledgeable, like Anli, needed to examine the connection of the iron bars to the window to see how best to remove them. And Charlotte might need a Healer. *If we find her.*

They crept across the roof, carefully scaling the

ridgepole and inched their way towards Charlotte's window. Square glass panes covered in cold black iron bars loomed out of the semi-darkness. Natalie grasped a bar, held on for dear life and tried to calm her galloping heart rate.

"Can you see anything?" she gasped.

"Nothing yet, we just got here. Give me a moment to look at this ironwork. Can you see Charlotte in there?"

Natalie peered into the room. It was dark except for a fireplace containing dimly glowing coals. Craning her neck Natalie couldn't see if anything or anyone was in there. She took a chance and made the slightest tapping sound on one pane of the glass with a fingernail.

She waited for an eternity. Charlotte didn't come to the window. Fortunately, neither did any guards or Ystrelle. Feeling braver Natalie knocked with her knuckle and then a small pocket knife she had taken to keeping in her leather bodice.

Blowing her hair out of her face, she put the pocketknife back. "If that doesn't get Charlotte's attention, I don't know what will," she muttered. "Any more and I'll aw—w—wake the entire palace." She closed her eyes and breathed through her nose. *Perhaps these speech issues are temporary. Please let it be so.*

"I've got it! Natalie, see what's connecting the bars to the window?" Anli pointed to a gray substance barely visible in the dawn light. "I've seen this before. I know I can remove it but we've got to get the right materials."

A ghostly form appeared at the window. Natalie jumped, her heart pounding anew. A wide-eyed face materialized from the darkness like a full moon. Silver hair falling to her elbows and dressed in a white shift, Charlotte, stared blankly out the window.

Natalie waved frantically. Charlotte's hands flew to her mouth and then to the windowsill, prying it up with her fingernails. Natalie tried to help from the outside but she couldn't get her arms through the iron bars at the correct angle to help.

Anli levered the window open with one of her daggers. The three women managed to open the window a few inches.

"Charlotte," Natalie cried in a whisper sticking her hands through the window.

Charlotte grabbed her fingers and kneeled down "Natalie you've got to go. Go, now."

"But we're here to rescue you."

"Don't rescue me, Natalie. Leave. Save yourselves."

"We'll be back. Anli knows how to get you out."

"I can't be saved Natalie. You have to go now."

Natalie quickly grounded herself accessing the ley lines radiating outward from the emerald megalith at the center of Ismereld. Directing this energy into her queen, she waited for it to create the blue limned outline of Charlotte's body in her mind.

It was a quick Naming, but Natalie had to see why Charlotte might be behaving like this; why she didn't want to be rescued. The images she saw the instant before Charlotte snatched her hand away made Natalie sick to her stomach.

"Natalie don't bother Healing me. I'm beyond saving." With one great heave, she slammed the window shut, turned and walked away.

CHAPTER 4

"Tell us what happened."

"Onlo, I can get her out," Anli lost everyone but him in a technical explanation of the materials holding the iron bars to the wall and what she needed to break Charlotte free.

"She warned us not to try to rescue her," Natalie interjected, swallowing back tears. "She told us quite bluntly to let her go. I was able to touch her and I could only do a brief Naming but... Goddess, what I saw ..." Natalie's voice broke.

Despite the coziness of the pub they'd chosen for breakfast, it was all Natalie could do to not burst into tears.

"Was she hurt?" Onlo asked.

"No, not physically," Natalie said, a tremor in her voice. "I think ... I think her body's fine but Ystrelle broke her mind somehow. I've never Named anyone and felt that feeling. It was the hollowest, most broken feeling I've ever felt in my life. Whatever has happened, it's enough that Charlotte does not want to endanger us."

Onlo swore.

"Well, we do have experience treating trauma. I'm certain, given time, we could try to Heal whatever Ystrelle did."

Natalie reached for Jules's hand and squeezed. "You're right. Let's get her back and help her."

If anyone knew about mental trauma, it would be Jules. Although not entirely recovered from his own mental and physical trauma at the hands of Healer Aldworth, he'd reached a point where life was livable. His trauma no longer overwhelmed him on a daily basis. When the memories did become too much to bear, Natalie helped him through the worst.

Jules was right, they could Heal Charlotte—if they had the opportunity.

"Right," she turned to Onlo and Anli. "What are your ideas for breaching the bars again?"

The door to the pub opened and a woman with long ink-black hair, kohl-lined mahogany eyes and henna-colored skin entered. All eyes in the pub turned to her.

The clicks of silverware on plates and the low hum of conversation stopped as the woman strode to the bar, chin high and shoulders back. She wore flowing robes that were a myriad of colors and sparkly gold bits. Although individually the colors didn't seem to go together, when taken as a whole, her robes were quite stunning.

She was one of the most extraordinary women Natalie had ever seen. It took her several seconds to comply with their standard procedure when anyone new came into a pub. She focused on her food kept one eye on the exits and the other on the newcomer.

Everyone tensed when the barkeep nodded and pointed the woman in their direction. Onlo and Anli reached for their daggers. Natalie discreetly slid her fingers down to the dagger she kept in her boot. *How did someone find us? We never visit the same pub twice.*

The woman approached their table, palms open and

facing them. "I come in peace."

No one at the table relaxed.

"Please hear me out. May I have a seat? I believe we share common interests regarding a person who shouldn't be in the palace." She looked meaningfully around the table.

Warily they all made room for her.

"Who are you and why are you here?" Jules demanded.

"My name is Geeta Ramesh and—"

The entire table gasped.

"I take it you know who I am," she said wryly.

"You're the Head Councilwoman of the Council of Isles," Natalie breathed.

"That's correct," she whispered. "Please let me order food so I can blend in. I have important news and a favor to ask."

Natalie sat on tenterhooks until the barkeep placed a steaming pile of scrambled eggs, bacon and a homemade roll in front of the Head Councilwoman.

"So," she said taking a bite and eying Natalie and Jules. "It's been a while since you've been to the Abbey."

Jules and Natalie nodded. "It's never been safe for us to go back," Natalie clarified.

After Healer Aldworth had exiled her and kidnapped Jules, he'd taken over the Abbey in place of the previous headmistress, Gayla. Uncertain how far Ystrelle's influence over Aldworth stretched, they hadn't ventured back to the Abbey after Aldworth's death.

"I'm here to ask you to return as Headmistress. The Abbey has fallen into disarray. After Gayla's death, it has no real leadership. The person trying to lead in her wake is trying, and failing miserably, to fill her shoes."

Natalie blinked. *Headmistress? Me?*

Jules swore. "No one is looking out for the students?"

"Not exactly," Geeta said. "I'm here to ask you both to return to the Abbey to see if you can fix the damage. It's in everyone's best interests for the Abbey to be a safe place for students of Healing. But I also need someone who knows what's really going on here in Roseharbor."

Jules rubbed his beard. "Ystrelle would seek to exploit the Abbey."

Natalie scrubbed her face with her palms. "It's not just the students and teachers. There's the library, too. If she decides to take away all the learning preserved there, or, Forve Fibid—Five Forbid—, destroy it..." Natalie took a deep breath, heat suffusing her face. *Yes, the best time for my speech issues to crop up is during a conversation with the Head Councilwoman of the Isles.*

"But we've also been trying to rescue the princess," Em pointed out.

"There may be a way to do both," Onlo interjected. "I have some ideas."

The Head Councilwoman inclined her head. "Before you finish your meal, I'd like to speak with Healer Desmond and Healer Rayvenwood alone, please."

Onlo and Anli rested hands on their weapons. The Head Councilwoman raised her hands once more. "You have every reason in the Isles to be suspicious. Believe me when I tell you that we want the same things and I mean no harm to Healers Desmond and Rayvenwood."

Natalie narrowed her eyes at the Head Councilwoman, trying to figure out if she was telling the truth. Her experience with council members and people in power thus far made her skeptical. Gayla, former Headmistress of the Abbey and Head Councilwoman of the Council of Healers, had been like a mother to her.

On the other hand, Healer Aldworth, her former mentor and also a member of the Council of Healers, had turned out to be a sociopathic killer. Ystrelle, the head of the Council of Master Gardeners was a power-hungry, delusional maniac. Even Guild Master Summerwood, head of the Special Operations Guild on Obfuselt, wasn't very good at her job.

But at least she wasn't a killer.

"I'm willing to talk to you alone but only where Onlo

and Anli can see us. You'll forgive us Head Councilwoman, but you are right. We have many reasons to doubt and I do not believe we are ready to give up these reasons now."

The Head Councilwoman inclined her dark head once again. "I accept your terms. Why don't we talk at the small table next to the window near the bar? I can explain what I need and your friends can keep an eye on you from here."

Jules and Natalie shared a glance. Jules took Natalie's hand and squeezed it. They turned to the Head Councilwoman. "All right."

Natalie stood and followed Head Councilwoman Geeta Ramesh across the pub. *What in the five Isles could the Head Councilwoman of the Council of Isles possibly want with Jules and me?*

CHAPTER 5

N atalie settled into the table with Jules and the Head Councilwoman, her stomach swooping and diving like seabirds catching fish.

"You know the Abbey has fallen into disarray following the loss of Headmistress Gayla," the Head Councilwoman said without preamble. "With deaths of Healers Aldworth and Hawkins, all three seats on the Council of Healers are empty—a void we must fill as soon as possible. You, Natalie, are my first nomination for the Council of Healers."

"You've got to be kidding," Natalie blurted out before remembering in whose company she sat.

A nomination for Headmistress for the Abbey was astonishing in and of itself. Consideration for the Council of Healers seemed like someone's deluded fantasy.

"Why me?"

"I'm very impressed with your and Healer Rayvenwood's accomplishments this past spring. I think you would make an excellent addition to the Council of Healers." She turned to Jules. "As for you Healer

Rayvenwood, I would like you to be the lead teacher of all the mages that the Special Operations Guild finds. I will have the Guild send all new mages to you.

"I would also like you to have a position on a Council. With mages re-emerging in our world, they will need leadership. A Council of Mages, perhaps."

Natalie glanced at Jules. Eyes wide, he stared at the Head Councilwoman, dumbfounded.

Natalie nodded her head vigorously. "That is a wise idea. Jules is older and has much more experience than I. He should have the position on both councils." Natalie interlaced her fingers and rested her chin on her knuckles. "Councilwoman, I'm only nineteen. It wasn't long ago that I my apprenticeship. Surely you should pick someone else."

The Head Councilwoman steepled her fingers and rested her hands on the table. "Yes, I could choose someone else. And, technically, you are correct; there are many Healers with more teaching and Healing experience than you. But, frankly, right now I don't know who to trust. I know I can trust people Gayla trusted—people already working to restore the proper monarch to the throne and take down Ystrelle. In short, Healer Desmond, I need *you*."

Natalie buried her head into her palms. She prayed the Head Councilwoman didn't think her actions were childish, but she desperately needed to escape the wise mahogany eyes considering her.

What is the woman thinking? I can name five Healers off the top of my head who would probably make better Headmistress and council woman than I would.

The warmth of the pub, so cheery when she walked in, suddenly seemed to smother her. The noise of the crowd enjoying their breakfast rose and crested like a wave. Although no customers had moved from their seats, all the bodies in the pub seemed to press in on her.

She breathed in through her nose. Every fiber of her being wanted to get up, walk out of the city and into a forest. Distance would lend clarity. And forests always eased her mind.

Jules rested his hand on her arm. "Natalie I think you should consider her nomination."

She dropped her hands to the table, pressing her lips shut. *He's kidding. Isn't he? Has living with his psychotic mother damaged his mind?*

A corner of Jules's mouth turned up. "No, I'm not kidding. Now, I might be a bit biased where you're concerned," he slid his hand into hers. His ardent emerald green gaze shot a bolt of warmth through her middle. "But during my work with you as a Healer this year, you've shown more intelligence, determination and leadership skills than any Healer I know.

"This proposal must be overwhelming. Perhaps don't answer her now; take some time to consider her offer."

Natalie slumped in her chair tears pricking her eyes. *Time. Ha. Would time even help?* When she'd come out of her coma, everyone—even herself—reassured her she'd get better with time.

She hadn't.

I'm weak. I'm not who I once was. Now there's two people telling me I could hold not one but two of the highest positions in the Isles. How could they even think her capable when she often couldn't recall words when she needed to? She'd lost so much physical stamina and ability thanks to the fatigue that threated to crush her very soul. Not to mention her head would randomly explode with migraines and she must cater to them, too.

What if she did accept their offer? How could she make a difference to the Abbey? To the Isles? How could she ensure the same corruption that turned her life upside down this year didn't take root ever again?

Natalie folded her arms on the table and dropped her forehead onto her arms, no longer caring what the Head Councilwoman thought of her manners.

Well, what if I just started with the Abbey? What if I updated the curriculum? Adding self-defense was a must. Honestly, she couldn't see why it wasn't taught in the first place. Healers often found themselves in the remote corners of Ismereld. Who knew what one might encounter?

Oh, an outdoor survival class, too. She never learned it and yet she found herself needing it this past spring. Luckily, she'd had Jules to teach her.

Ooo, she and Jules could teach their method of Healing in a pair to other people. That way, Healing would be more accessible to those who couldn't use two hands.

She sat back, put her thumbnail in her mouth and started chewing on it. Over the years, Healers had gotten too used to the snug, safe conditions of the Abbey. But as she had found out this past year, Healers could do anything but rest on their laurels; they needed to be ready for anything. If she could make a difference in that, so much the better.

As for being a Councilwoman … she didn't know the first thing about the position. "Head Councilwoman, what do members of the Council of Isles do? Let's say I accept the position. I know I would have to attend Council meetings with representatives from the other Isles; what else would I do?"

A wry smile graced the Head Councilwoman's lips. "Thankfully, it's not all meetings. A member of the Council of Healers has a big say in Healer policy, not only as it applies to Ismereld citizens, but people coming from other Isles and even the continent. You are also in charge of reviews when Healer conduct or decisions are called into question."

Natalie gave her braid a savage twist at the memory of her own reviews. There were about five-thousand things she'd change about reviews if she had any say.

"You could also try to make inroads with Roseharbor society to alter their perception of Healers," the Head Councilwoman continued. You would be, after all, their equal or better as a Councilwoman."

Natalie and Jules snorted at the thought of Roseharbor society considering Healers as anything other than the lowest trade.

"You'll never know unless you try."

Try? That's all I've been doing for the last two months. Trying *to recover.* Trying *to speak without mixing up words.* Trying *to get better from headache after headache. And to what end? I am not much better than when I came out of the coma. "Trying" does not magically solve problems just because you do it.*

"I believe Healer Rayvenwood is correct. You should take some time to think this over. Meet me at the Mellow Harp Tavern tomorrow at five in the evening. You can tell me your decision about Headmistress then. Sorry for the short notice, but there's no time to spare. The Abbey needs help as soon as possible. If you do take the position, I will visit the Abbey in one month. You can let me know about your decision to be a Councilwoman then."

With that, Head Councilwoman Geeta Ramesh stood, thanked them both and swept from the pub, leaving Natalie staring at Jules, bewildered.

CHAPTER 6

"This is amazing," Jules exclaimed. "I already have hundreds of things I'd like to add to the curriculum for beginner mages. I'll have to send for the notes you and Em took during our lessons with Jyrenn this past summer. I'm sure Guild Master Summerwood kept them safe on Obfuselt. That way, I won't have to recall everything from memory."

Jules described his plans for the future in great detail, gesticulating as he talked and struggling to keep his voice low. Even though she was preoccupied with her own thoughts, Natalie couldn't help but be amused by his enthusiasm.

He stopped and stared at her quizzically. "Nat? You don't seem excited about this."

"Jules, she just asked me to be an honest to Goddess leader. I've only really led six people. And look how that turned out." She stared over his shoulder at the rays of sunlight streaming through the window.

This past summer, it was she who had led the six of them

to Roseharbor. She'd been so certain she, Jules, Anli, Onlo, Em and Charlotte could abort the nefarious plans of Healer Aldworth and de-throne Charlotte's corrupt parents. Instead, they'd lost Charlotte to Ystrelle and barely escaped with their lives.

Blinking, she returned her eyes to Jules's emerald gaze. "Now suddenly the Head Councilwoman of the bloody Council of Isles wants me to take on the entire Abbey. Jules, how can I fill Gayla's shoes? I'm still having problems speaking."

"You'll be—"

"Please don't tell me I'll be fine. I appreciate your support, I do, and I know you believe in me. But I can't do this unless I believe in myself. My head is broken, Jules. If I can't f-fi-fix myself, how can I fix our home?" Natalie shook her head, a sob welling up in her throat.

Jules put his hand on her arm. "We'll all be there to help put the Abbey back together."

"I know I can count on all of you. That's not my worry. The staff and students need to respect me; look up to me. Think of the authority Gayla commanded; surely I cannot command that same authority when I can't even think of the right word a lot of the time. How can I physically do her job when I still need to nap every day? I feel very honored by the Head Councilwoman's offer, but all I foresee is me feeling stupid and embarrassed all the time."

Jules moved to Natalie's side, picked her up and set her in his lap. Enfolding her in his arms, he brushed his lips across her temple. "I wish I hadn't taken that last shot during the palace battle."

"Please don't blame yourself. I don't. We had to get out of there somehow. When you think back, it's amazing we escaped that throne room at all. I mean, Healer Aldworth had just killed the king and queen and then Ystrelle started talking about starting a breeding program for mages using you and Charlotte." She shook her head. "No, we had to get out of there. You did what you had to do. Using me as a source of mage energy was an experimental technique. We learned the hard way that it is most certainly not something you should include in your new curriculum."

Jules ran his hand down her back. "That we did. I just wish you didn't have to pay the price."

"And I wish you never had to pay the price for Aldworth's grief over his dead wife, but here we are. There's nothing to be done about it. Just two broken people trying to right some wrongs."

Jules gently pushed Natalie's shoulders back and caught her gaze. "You're *not* broken. Do you think I am broken?"

Natalie blinked at him. "No, but—"

"Everyone's body and mind is different—"

"Now you're talking about differences from birth," Natalie protested.

He shook his head. "Even after we're born, differences become a part of us all. The bodies we have get injured or sick. They break down, sometimes even before we get old. But that shouldn't stop us from living. Look at me. Or think of Aaron."

"Aaron? But my brother is fine."

"He fell out of an apple tree and got a concussion when he was five, didn't he? If that head injury had paralyzed him from the legs down, wouldn't you move heaven and earth to make sure he had the same opportunities he would have had otherwise?"

"Of course I would. But this is different. This fatigue; it's not just tiredness. It's *bone-crushing*. Each of our spy missions leaves me so exhausted, I feel like my body is filled with sand. I could fall on the floor and never get up again. I used to be able to train in self-defense with Onlo for two hours. Now, I'm lucky if I can do anything."

"Natalie, you're stubborn and strong. If anyone can figure out how to put the Abbey back together, even while experiencing these symptoms, it's you. You wouldn't let me quit Healing when I lost my hand," he cupped the side of her face, caressing her cheek with his thumb. "I'm not going to let you give up now."

Gathered around the kitchen table at Rayvenwood House that evening, Natalie finished telling the story of Head Councilwoman Ramesh's proposals to her friends.

"What do you think?" she concluded morosely.

Onlo shrugged. "We're certainly not getting a lot done here. I think it's time to draw Ystrelle out. She must know we're in the city after the Queensguard spotted us yesterday. So we go to the Abbey. Not only can you take on your new role, but chances are she'll come for us; maybe we can use that."

Natalie gaped at him. "Is that really a good idea?"

"We've been here for a month Natalie," Anli put in. "We finally got to Charlotte last night. I can tell you the technology we'll need to get those bars off is pretty significant. We need a safe place and time to plan. Speaking of which, we need to start packing before Jules's lovely mother pays us a visit."

Jules rolled his eyes. "Unfortunately, that's true. Roseharbor is about an hour's ride from the Abbey. Natalie, you, Em and I can return to the Abbey put things back in order. Onlo, you and Anli can travel back and forth between Roseharbor and the Abbey as needed."

"I still can't believe she wants me to be ..." Natalie swallowed past the lump in her throat as her brain once more refused to supply the word she needed. The silence dragged on as her friends looked on her with kindness. "Headmistress," she managed at last *Thanks, brain. Please do emphasize that I'm not qualified for the job.*

"It's a lot to take in," Jules grasped her hand and smiled at her. "Let's start packing so we can return to the Abbey. Anli's right, we—"

A voice boomed from the stairs. "Juliers Rayvenwood. Are you leaving for that wretched Abbey again?"

Jules rubbed his forehand with his hand. "Mother, go

away. This does not concern you. We thank you for your—hospitality—but it's time for us to go now."

"No," she marched down the stairs her silk-covered bejeweled shoes stamping on the floor. "You will not leave the city until you marry Charlotte. I *will* see my son on the throne."

Jules stood up from the table. "I regret ever coming here," he said under his breath. Turning to face the woman who gave birth to him, he said: "Mother when are you going to learn that I am not your puppet. I never have been and I never will be."

"No, you are my son you will do as your father and I tell you."

"Mother I am twenty-six years old. Enough."

"Your father and I have worked for decades raising our family to one of the highest stations in Roseharbor society. You will not undo it by running back to that Abbey with this low born wh—"

Natalie blinked and stared agape at Jules's mother. Everyone else at the table stood up; Onlo's fingertips brushed one of his daggers.

Jules stalked to his mother until he was nearly nose to nose with her, a muscle twitching in his jaw. "Choose your next words carefully, Mother. Apologize to Natalie. Right now."

Victoria Rayvenwood's eyes narrowed. "Your father was right to disown you. Whatever was I thinking taking you back in my home? Get out."

"With pleasure," Jules whirled away from her and stormed out the kitchen door. His mother proceeded regally up the stairs, chin held high using the tips of her fingers to hold her dress so she wouldn't step on it.

"I'll be glad to see the back of that thrice-damned woman," Em glared at the empty stairway leading upstairs.

"You and me both, my love," Anli said.

Natalie's heart pounded in her ears, fingertips gripping the table as if it was the only thing holding her onto the earth. Growing up as she did on an apple farm in Mistfell and then at the Abbey, she'd never been exposed to any sort of class system or social strata. Roseharbor was the first place she'd ever encountered any sort of prejudice for who she was or where she came from.

To think I used to believe the capital of the Five Isles would be a shining example of all the Isles stand for. Looking out for each other. Valuing people for their talents and not their birth. I couldn't have been more wrong.

The door to the kitchen slammed once more announcing Jules's return. He strode across the room, face ablaze. He kneeled on one knee beside her. "Natalie Desmond I apologize for the behavior of my mother."

"Jules, it's not your fault."

"That may be, but you deserve an apology. And you'll never get one from her. Let's go home. Go home for good."

"I'd love to, but I ... I'm not ready. I don't know what to do," she covered her face with her hands. "We can't stay here but I can't go home. Not yet. Not now. I need time to think." She reached for Jake under the table, hugging his neck as he put his forepaws on his lap. "I want to go for a walk in the woods. It's too crowded here."

"All right. We'll leave."

"We will?" Anli rounded on Jules. Where will we go? Since you're not brave enough to go to the Abbey yet, Miss Healer—"

Oh, good, I'm on Anli's bad side again. Didn't take much. Just some self-doubt—or self-pity—because of my brain injury. And just after Jules's mother called me a whore. Perfect timing.

"Anli, can you just—"

"No. No, I can't just. One visit from the Head Councilwoman and suddenly our mission isn't about Charlotte at all. It's about her," she jabbed a finger at Natalie.

"Anli, love, that's unfair," Em put in.

"Is it?"

Jules held out a hand. "No one is suggesting we abandon

our quest to rescue Charlotte.

"But you would make it that much harder by going Goddess knows where while Natalie makes up her mind."

Jules raised his voice to match Anli's. "She deserves all the time we can give her to decide if she wants to accept the Head Councilwoman's offers."

"Then go take it," Anli shouted back.

Jules snatched Natalie's hand. "We will. Please do stay here with my devil of a mother. I hope you're happy together."

Natalie stood, following Jules to the room they shared off the kitchens, the unusual sound of Em and Anli arguing following them down the hallway.

"Jules," she hissed. "What are you doing?"

"Giving you time. Time away."

"H-how?"

"We're leaving. Just us."

"But it's cold outside."

He squeezed her hand. "I'll keep you warm."

CHAPTER 7

Natalie twisted the end of her braid as she peered out at the thick, fluffy snowflakes twirling down from the forest canopy.

"I can hear you worrying from here."

She snapped the tent flap closed. "It's awfully early in the fall for the first snow, don't you think? Will it snow a lot? I've never had to survive outdoors in the snow."

Rising from his bedroll and drawing her close, Jules rested his chin on her head. Jake padded over and curled up in a tight ball on her feet, nose tucked under the fluffy part of his tail. "Do you remember when you had to get me from this forest to the palace while I was unconscious, vomiting and feverish? And in the pouring rain, I might add."

Natalie rolled her eyes. She knew why Jules kept trying to remind her of her accomplishments. But it all seemed so far away. Like another person had done all those things.

"Did the walk here help you make a decision at all?"

They'd been forced to leave their horses—who'd belonged to Jules's family—behind at Rayvenwood House.

That morning's hike from the wealthy neighborhoods on the outskirts of Roseharbor to the forests outside the city had drained all of Natalie's little energy. She'd gratefully slept while Jules hunted for their dinner.

Despite her body protesting much of the way, the crunch of the brown leaves beneath her feet, the smell of snow in the air and the sight of Jake bounding over fallen trees was exactly what she needed.

"I haven't come to a decision yet. But I feel like I have room to make one now. I don't feel … surrounded by so much pressure."

Jules squeezed her. "Anli laid it on a little thick didn't she?"

"Yeah. At least I never have to wonder what she's thinking."

"I wish you could've met my sister, Priscilla, while we were in Roseharbor. You never have to wonder what she's thinking either, only she's nicer about it."

Natalie snuggled into Jules's chest. "Tell me about her."

"Well, at first glance, she looks like an eight-year-old princess's birthday cake brought to life. The dresses she wears are large, pink, and have a lot of lace and layers. She often seems vapid to a lot of people, and she can bat her eyelashes behind a fan at a ball with the best of them. But I know better. We grew up and had to survive Mother and Father together. She adjusted to Roseharbor society much better than I."

Natalie shuddered. "I can't imagine ever getting used to such strictures and expectations."

"Father always wanted me to take over for him and be a master tailor. Priscilla is rather wretched at sewing, but she really has an eye for design. He never saw her talent, just as he never saw my calling as a Healer."

Natalie yawned. "If you two get along so well, why didn't we go stay with her instead of your parents?"

"She and her husband, Woodes, live in Roseharbor proper, in one of the townhouses in the wealthy part of the city. I didn't think it would be safe for us there, and I didn't want to bring any trouble down on them from our spying activities. At least where Mother and Father's house is, there's a chance to lose someone who might be following you."

Natalie turned her head so her cheek touched his. "I'm sorry your parents are so…"

"Horrible? Narrow-minded? Cold?"

She could feel Jules's grin against her cheek. "Unsupportive. Unaware of the wonderful son they have."

Jules squeezed her. "And I'm sorry you had to experience the receiving end of Mother's wrath."

"It was … shocking. I'm not used to people, let alone the mother of the man I love, using my birth against me. But it helped that everyone leaped right to my defense. Plus, it doesn't matter. Not really."

Jules nuzzled her hair. "Mmm?" Jules trailed a string of kisses from her hair down her jawline. "And what does matter, my love?"

"That we love each other," she whispered huskily, and then turned and captured his mouth with hers, threading her fingers through his dark, wavy hair.

Finally, we're away from his mother and the servants. We're not crammed in with our friends. We're alone in the middle of a snowstorm.

"I'll keep you warm," he'd promised. Judging by the delicious heat pooling in her belly and working its way lower, Jules intended to keep his vow.

She surrendered herself to the tide of sensations washing over her, falling backwards with Jules onto the bedrolls. Digging her fingernails into his scalp, she pulled him close. His lips left hers to trace her eyebrows while his fingers left trails of heat on her throat, inching down to the laces at the top of her shirt.

Unable to stop herself, Natalie yawned. Jules's deep laugh filled the tent.

"That boring am I?"

"No! I'm so sorry, I—"

"Hush, love. We pushed your body so much today. Never think I don't understand." He pulled her bedroll over her and Jake and planted a chaste kiss on her forehead. "Get some rest."

Natalie turned onto her side, snuggled back against Jules, threw a leg over Jake and was asleep before Jules blew out the lantern.

Natalie donned the boots Onlo gave her this past summer, thankful for the rabbit fur lining she'd added. Drawing her long, wool, emerald green Healer's cloak about her, she stepped out of the tent into the early morning light shining on the new fallen snow.

Her feet crunched slowly through the forest. She breathed with every step, observing the snowfall on the branches, the sound of the snow falling off the trees and hitting the ground, the feel of the snow under her boots and the tingling tips of her fingers.

Jake seemed oblivious to the cold, bounding in silly looking hops through the forest. Natalie could already see balls of snow forming in the long hair on his legs. She wrinkled her nose; it would be a big job getting those out later on.

But at last she was finally alone.

I appreciate Jules's support. I really do. But if I'm going to do this, I need to believe in myself. And I don't. Too much has gone wrong. I've made too many mistakes.

Her mindful walk through the snow became a slow trudge, shoulders slumped, eyes unfocused. Her toe caught on a branch; she tripped and nearly fell. Catching herself on a nearby tree, she pushed herself upright and glared at the offending piece of wood, which she'd dislodged from under the snow.

Bending down, she picked it up with both hands. It was almost the same length as the short staffs she had learned to use so well over the summer. She twirled the branch experimentally, her body remembering what it felt like to have mastery of a physical skill.

She'd learned self-defense skills after Aldworth had exiled her from Ismereld, stripped of her Healer status and kidnapped Jules. *I took a long time to decide about learning self-defense, too. I was so concerned about hurting others and being a Healer. That the two could not be reconciled. But in the end I discovered a skill I loved and valued. And it saved me and my friends lives.*

And now she couldn't even make it through the second sequence of the *reiqata*, Obfuselt's ancient martial arts system. At Rayvenwood House, she'd often rested atop dark blue silk cushions in a secluded bay window seat. The sight of Onlo and Anli sparring outside was enough to squash her heart into pieces and leave her in tears.

She considered the staff in her hand. "Gayla, what would you say? What would you tell me to do?"

Natalie waited, watching her breath make clouds in the frigid air.

Gayla didn't answer. No one did.

She changed the orientation of the staff, put one end on the ground and leaned on it. Onlo would have had her head had she done this in weapons practice. But her body needed support now.

Her body needed more things, in fact, than it ever had in her life. Was there time and energy left to oversee the Abbey?

"In short, Healer Desmond, I need you," the Head Councilwoman had said. And Natalie's brain did overflow with ideas for the Abbey. But surely the woman Geeta Ramesh needed was the Healer Desmond who stopped an epidemic and had the same disease named after her.

Desmond's Fever. By the Five, I still hate that name.

The Head Councilwoman probably didn't need *this* Healer Desmond who stood in the frozen woods mourning all she'd lost.

Natalie exhaled a big puff of air and recalled the day she and Jules left to investigate the epidemic in Whitestrand.

She'd ridden a short, chestnut pony named Benji. He was her favorite in the Abbey stables. Unfortunately, he'd done nothing to boost her confidence riding next to Jules, tall and regal on his shiny bay gelding.

My confidence was low then, too. After my patient went into a coma and was paralyzed during my apprenticeship, my confidence was so shaky. I thought it was my fault for so long.

She gripped her staff even tighter. This past spring—less than a year, but somehow a lifetime ago—the Abbey had needed her. She hadn't believed in herself one bit, but she'd come through and stopped the epidemic in Roseharbor.

Jake ran up to her and jumped up, placing his snowy paws on her waist. A small mound of snow sat on his nose and his eyes sparkled even in the gray morning. Grinning, Natalie took one hand off her staff and scratched the fur around his neck. *Well, I stopped the epidemic with help from my friends. Maybe ... maybe I can govern the Abbey, too. With more help.*

She waited to see if there was some sign that her decision was the right one. Perhaps a sort of click in her heart like a broken bone going back into place or the clouds parting and the sun shining through into the forest.

Instead, all that happened was Jake farting as he removed his paws from her person and dragged his rear end on the ground.

Natalie grasped her staff, peals of laughter echoing through the forest. *Silly dog. I think I will meet the Head Councilwoman at the Mellow Harp Tavern tonight and agree to be Headmistress.*

"The Abbey might not be the home we remember anymore, Jake. I think we're going to find quite a mess when we get there. Five willing, I'll be able to fix it."

CHAPTER 8

The dappled shade of the forest gave way to full sunlight as Natalie rounded the corner and beheld the Abbey. Large and imposing, its gray stone walls rose toward the sky as if it had grown out of the ground eons ago. Tall, narrow windows with rounded tops punctuated the thick walls. Despite its cold, imposing exterior, Natalie had always found the Abbey bright and warm on the inside.

Fall painted the trees dotting the rolling hills surrounding the Abbey bright oranges, yellows and reds. Breathing in the familiar scents of the forest was akin to smelling homemade bread baking in Mother's kitchen.

"Well, the building isn't on fire and no one is running amok. Maybe the whole thing is abandoned."

Onlo snorted. "We haven't been inside yet."

"I hope Cook is still here," Em wished. "Wait until you taste her iced cinnamon raisin buns."

Anli put a hand on her stomach. "Em, love, don't talk about food, I'm starving."

The stables, thankfully, weren't abandoned. The stable master, Bonnie, a petite woman with chin length gray hair and leathery skin from a life spent outdoors, took their horses and set about untacking, grooming and feeding them with her usual meticulous care.

Clutching the letter from the Council of Isles announcing her as the official new Headmistress of the Abbey in her fist, Natalie approached the front door of her home with her friends at her back. Pushing open the large wooden door, she blinked in the dim foyer, and inhaled the first smell of home since last spring.

She strode into Gayla's office and her hand flew to her mouth. "Oh my Goddess."

Someone had searched the room—a long time ago by the looks of it. Gayla's books littered the floor, the ancient bookshelves covered in cobwebs. The pieces of her antique tea sets lay scattered around like dried bones. Drying herbs no longer covered the walls; they'd been torn down and left in piles making the floor look like a garden someone had forgotten to weed. Ink stained paper lay strewn all over the desk and the surrounding floor.

"What are you doing in here?" a voice from behind her demanded.

Natalie whirled. "Who are you?"

A tall man with short chestnut hair and impeccably tailored clothing stepped into the dim light shed by the cobwebbed windows. "I'm Healer Brendon Edmundson. Once again, who are you?"

"Who's in charge here?" Natalie queried, putting her hands on her hips. Judging from the way Healer Edmundson's cloak swished dramatically behind him, she had a strong suspicion.

"A few months ago Headmistress Gayla died. I am in charge now."

Natalie lifted her chin and held up her letter and resisted the bizarre urge to apologize. "Not anymore. I'm here to replace her by order of Geeta Ramesh, Head

Councilwoman of the Isles."

He looked as if he'd just found something unpleasant on the bottom of his boot. "I don't believe you."

Natalie held his gaze, her face expressionless, letter extended toward him.

Giving in to the pressure of the staring contest first, Healer Edmundson snatched the letter from her, opened it and began to read. He raised his eyebrows at her over the paper. "Desmond as in Desmond's Fever?"

Natalie ground her teeth and ignored the smiles of her friends. "Yes."

"I expected someone older. Not someone so childish as to dye her hair such a childish shade of red."

Anli snorted.

"Well, you have me. And the dye was necessary at the time. It will fade soon enough. You may know Healers Juliers Rayvenwood and Emmeline Arnold?"

Healer Edmundson glanced at Jules and Em, and then back to her. "Why are you here now?"

"We've been trying to rescue Queen Charlotte." Natalie proceeded to fill him in on the true details of the transfer of power that occurred in Roseharbor.

"You want me to believe three Healers—you three, in point of fact—have been working to restore the throne? With two people from Obfuselt? Ridiculous."

"It's true whether you believe it or not. Now, tell me what is the status here?"

"I've got everything under control."

"That's not what we hear."

Healer Edmundson's face turned blotchy red. "And what *do* you hear?" he ground out.

Unwilling to make an enemy on her first day back to the Abbey, Natalie held up both hands in a gesture of peace. "Look, you've been running things since Gayla passed away. The Head Councilwoman wants me to step in as Headmistress. Let's see if we can work together."

"I'm going to verify this letter with the Council of Isles.

I don't see why I need to work with you."

So much for peacemaking. "Go right ahead," Natalie said to his retreating back. The moment he was out of the room, she let out a breath. "That was fun. Let's go up to the classrooms. I want to see what's going on. "

Most of the classrooms were empty: desks, chairs and papers abandoned. Only a few professors still ran classes for a disappointingly small number of students. Each professor walked among their students, shoulders slumped, with dark circles under their eyes.

Jules stood in one empty classroom. "Where are the students?"

Natalie ran her finger along a desk and glared at the dark gray mound of dust on her finger tip. "I don't know. I will most assuredly find out."

"Let's try the dormitories," Em suggested. But the long stone corridors lined with dark wooden doors echoed with only their footsteps and voices.

"Likely they've gone down to Saltwick for a pint," Anli suggested.

"Or five. From the look of things, they can go down to Saltwick anytime and stay as long as they like," Onlo commented dryly.

Leaving the dormitory wing and heading toward the cloisters, Natalie's heart sped up. *Please, Goddess, let my—the Abbey's—greenhouse still be there.*

A swarm of memories assaulted Natalie. Walking into the greenhouse's magical interior for the first time when she was thirteen. Endless afternoons spent blissfully tending and preparing medicinal plants beneath its foggy glass roof. Healers coming to her to prepare or cultivate a needed plant.

She tried to open the door; when it wouldn't open, she peered in one window.

"It's barred shut. Why would someone bar the door to a greenhouse? And how did they do it from the inside and get out again?"

Onlo stepped up beside her and broke the bar with one

swift kick. "Let's find out," he gestured for her to walk ahead of him.

Swallowing back tears, she stepped over the threshold.

Her worktable sat on its side, keeled over like an abandoned boat. The plants grew wild, weeds standing among them anxious for the opportunity to take over. Brown spots, scale and holes in leaves abounded; clearly a variety of insects made a regular meal of the greenhouse contents.

Gently, Natalie pushed the overgrown plants back and entered the drying room. All the harvested herbs were either piled on the floor or on the table in a heap of dried flowers and leaves. Natalie covered her nose when the stench of rot became overwhelming. Peering up, she spied a water stain on the wooden ceiling. *Well. I suppose no one would care enough to repair the ceiling of some place that's been trashed.*

Returning to the main greenhouse, Natalie swallowed past the large lump in her throat. "There's nothing here that can't be salvaged."

Moving on to the library, they found a morass of dust and cobwebs. Books littered the floor and shelves hung at odd angles, the empty spaces standing out like a mouth full of empty teeth.

"It's like seeing holy ground desecrated," Jules murmured.

Natalie pursed her lips and added finding the librarian, Healer Misaki, to her mental to-do list. She prayed the young woman was safe.

Last up was the hospital. This facet of the Abbey, at least, was much as they'd left it. Bandages, jars, surgical supplies and more stood in neat rows on the supply closet shelves. Healers tended patients in neatly made beds in the main hospital room.

It was obvious where Healer Edmundson had focused all of his efforts.

Natalie whirled and leveled her gaze at the surrounding people. "There will be a meeting in the Great Hall tonight;

Healers and students alike. Jules and Em, spread the word amongst the staff. Onlo, Anli, ride to Saltwick, find all the students you can, and do the same. I have a few words to say."

CHAPTER 9

Carefully setting her candle down on Gayla's desk that night, Natalie sank to the floor and at last allowed a few tears to spill down her cheeks. She picked up a few of Gayla's old papers, paging through them to see if they contained anything important.

I can't believe this is my office now. How can I possibly counsel students the way Gayla did? Anytime I came to her, I knew I could count on tea and wisdom: whether I wanted to hear it or not.

A number of people in the Great Hall had heard a tough message from Natalie themselves earlier this evening. She had announced the Council of the Isles' decision to make her Headmistress to numerous sounds of surprise and dismay. No one bothered to conceal their whispers of "She's not old enough," "Didn't she just graduate?" or "I hear she was exiled."

Natalie raised her voice above the whispers. "This is how it is. Classes will resume tomorrow and attendance is mandatory. I will take over the assignment of hospital shifts and the assignment of staff. In between classes and hospital shifts we are all, as a school, going to clean up the library. Knowledge is our sacred resource and therefore the responsibility of every single one of us.

"I miss Headmistress Gayla fiercely, but she is not coming back. I'm sure I have a long way to go before I earn your respect. Until then, your cooperation is my expectation."

When her audience filed out of the Great Hall, the silence threated to suffocate Natalie. Clenching her fists behind her back, she swore with every strange look and mutter that she would get the Abbey back up and running; she owed it to Headmistress Gayla.

Healer Edmundson glared daggers at her from across the room. She doubted she would ever win him over, but if he followed her directions she would settle for that.

Attempting to return her attention to contents of her former Headmistress's papers, she wondered idly what Gayla had faced upon becoming Headmistress; had anyone doubted or challenged her? If so, how had she earned the respect of so many? *If only she were here to tell me.*

Natalie's thoughts kept her company as she sorted through the debris, throwing into the fire anything that was no longer needed or salvageable. She repaired the bookshelves and carefully put the books she'd been able to save back where they belonged.

She shed a few more tears as she swept up the tea sets with which she and Gayla used to take tea. Natalie grabbed her black leather-bound notebook that she'd gotten in Obfuselt when she started teaching Healing to Charlotte and added to her ever-growing to-do list to purchase a new tea set and some tea.

Bits of floor were just beginning to show when she came across a large book bound in brown leather and filled with yellowed pages. Natalie flipped through the sketches within, mouth agape. Astonishingly lifelike depictions of students learning and teachers at work at the Abbey filled each page. Carefully turning the aged paper, Natalie didn't recognize anyone; judging by the dates carefully marked in the corners of the sketches, it was obvious Gayla had been chronicling life at the Abbey with painstaking care for years.

Towards the back she found sketches of people she knew, including herself. One drawing depicted her at work in the greenhouse, bare feet in the dirt and grinding some unknown substance with the mortar and pestle. There was one of Jules teaching a room full of children, his youthful face filled with enthusiasm, his expressive hands helping convey the concept he was teaching. There was a sketch of Em, skillfully bringing a child into the world with the calm and confidence that made her the favorite of so many expectant mothers.

Closing the book carefully, Natalie gave it a place of honor on the bookshelves.

Gayla, I know you're with the Goddess now, but I will do my best to be everything you knew I could be. And more.

CHAPTER 10

At breakfast the next morning, Natalie kept her shoulders back and her face serene, determined no one in the Great Hall would know a flock of butterflies careened around her stomach.

Fortunately, the cook, a short woman with her chestnut hair swept back into a loose bun, had kept the kitchens running. A corner of Natalie's mouth turned up. This did not surprise her in the least; Cook was not a woman to cross. She remembered her heart beating as fast as a small bird's when she and Em would sneak into the kitchen during a night of studying to grab a snack.

The morning bells tolled in the bell tower. Students went to their first classes, some eagerly and others dragging their feet and shooting Natalie spiteful looks. She kept her chin up and met their gazes evenly. Let them try to cross her; she'd faced worse than surly students.

She patrolled the halls with Jules and Jake that morning, making sure all was in order. She'd set up shifts of teachers to patrol Saltwick for anyone skipping class. She hadn't made any changes to Healer Edmundson's staffing. Yet.

The sight of teachers walking amongst students in classrooms was a complete change from their arrival yesterday. Trading a grin, Natalie and Jules walked toward Gayla's—her—office.

"Let's review the class schedules to make sure that the right teachers are teaching the right classes. We need to make room in the school day for your mage classes. I take it you've been working on a curriculum, Mage Rayvenwood?"

"Oh, be quiet."

She snorted with laughter and squeezed his hand. His excitement and enthusiasm for his new role was a balm to her soul.

Healer Edmundson marched up to them as they entered the Abbey foyer. "I had it all in hand, *Headmistress*."

Natalie arched an eyebrow. "Did you? Then why were so many students absent from class? Why is the m-library a mess? Why is Gayla's office trashed, and the greenhouse overgrown like an abandoned garden in someone's backyard?"

"You will soon see how difficult it is to manage an operation as large as the Abbey. I doubt you can do better. You may have stopped the epidemic, but that doesn't make you qualified to be Headmistress." With that he strode on down the hallway.

Natalie's stomach churned. Gritting her teeth, she closed her office door behind herself and Jules.

Jules rubbed his forehead. "Well, he is a fine piece of work, isn't he? He was a classmate of mine and was a stuck up, arrogant ass even then."

Natalie winked at him. "Sounds like someone I used to know."

Jules threw a quill at her, which Natalie caught deftly. They sat and got to work evaluating the current class schedule, reassigning teachers as needed.

Biting the end of her quill, Natalie studied their chart. "A lot of people are not going to like this."

Jules shook his head. "No." However, one side of his mouth turned up in a lopsided grin.

"Why are you so pleased?"

"I like the idea of turning this whole place on its head. Not only do we have a chance to restore the order Gayla kept, but we have a chance to improve upon what she did."

Natalie buried her face in her hands "I just need to be able to face these teachers and students. They need to respect me. Why would they do that? *I'm* not even confident I can do this, Jules. Everyone loves to tell me how amazing it is that I figured out the source of the epidemic. But it's just one of the very few accomplishments to date in my life. For Goddess's sake, I'm only nineteen. Healer Edmundson is right. People won't respect me."

Jules sat back in his chair and ran a hand over his chin. "They *listened* to you this morning. They went back to class. You certainly won't earn their respect overnight, but with consistency and good decisions, I know you'll earn it over time."

"Do we have time? Ystrelle must know we're here by now. We still need to get Charlotte out of that palace. We still need to—"

Jules put up a hand. "One thing at a time, Natalie. Let's start with the class schedule and cleaning up the library."

Meeting the first group of students and teachers in the library after lunch, Natalie gave basic instructions. "It's pretty simple. All we have to do is put the shelves back on the books and—"

The students glanced at one another and some hid giggles behind their hands. Natalie blinked, realizing her brain had messed up the words.

She pursed her lips together into something she hoped resembled a smile. "I suffered a brain injury about two months ago. I've recovered well, though I still get headaches and often mix up words. Even with my lingering symptoms, I can assure you I'm quite up to the task." Whether the task was cleaning the library or being Headmistress, she didn't specify.

She took a deep breath and tried the sentence again. "All we have to do is put the books back on the shelves. As we go, let's give the place a thorough dusting. This place used to feel like home; let's make it do so again."

The volunteers took rags and polish and began. Natalie took a cloth and some polish for herself and set to work alongside them.

"Have you tried rubbing half a lemon on your forehead?"

Natalie blew stray wisps of hair out of her face and glanced up at the Healer working alongside her. "I'm sorry, what?"

"Half a lemon on your forehead when the headaches come? I prescribe it to all my headache patients."

Natalie looked at her askance. "What professor taught you this? Would I Activate the lemon?"

"Oh, I didn't learn this here. A man in my home town used to use this remedy every time he had a headache—any time we could get lemons, that is."

"No. No, I haven't tried this."

"You should. It always worked for him."

"Hmm," was Natalie's only reply.

It always worked for him. How? And if so why would it work for someone else? Had any Healer tried this on a large group patients and observed the effects?

Natalie thought of Manuel, the plant scientist on Solerin, working on his meticulous experiments in his massive greenhouse. She doubted he ever jumped to conclusions based on one tale from his home town.

A lemon on the forehead for a headache. What will they come up with next?

With a week's worth of work, the library started to look like itself again. The shelves gleamed and the books, freshly clean of dust, stood side by side in colorful rows. Every nook and cranny was cobweb-free.

Natalie surveyed the space with pride, one hand on her hip holding her rag. When her headaches and fatigue forced her to curl up in bed, she'd remember this small victory.

A bright-eyed curly-haired girl approached Natalie, twisting her dress in her hands. "Healer, I mean, Headmistress Desmond?"

Natalie swallowed as she estimated the girl approaching her fifth year at the Abbey and nearly about to start her apprenticeship; not that much younger than Natalie herself.

"Yes, what's your name, sweeting?"

"McKenna, Headmistress."

"Are we all finished? It certainly looks so much better than it did." Perspiration beaded on McKenna's almond-colored skin and a deep flush covered her high cheek bones.

"You're absolutely right McKenna, we've done a great job. I think we'll move on to the greenhouse next."

McKenna's face lit with excitement. "I love the greenhouse. I know you used to work in the greenhouse a lot. I thought I might try to keep it up when you were gone but someone barred the door. I didn't want to chance getting in trouble. Since Headmistress Gayla died, it was like all the rules changed." McKenna bit her lip and looked over Natalie's shoulder.

"Come with me for a moment, if you would, please." Natalie looped her arm around the younger girl's and gently led her to an out-of-the-way table in the library. "I'm sorry, the only chance I've had to talk with students since returning is about disciplinary issues. I haven't had a chance to speak with students who are doing well."

McKenna blushed.

"What was it like while we were gone?"

"I hated it," McKenna blurted out, glancing around before continuing. "I dreamed of going to school here since

57

I was a little girl. My first few years here were the best years of my life. And then ... Headmistress Gayla died."

McKenna picked at a knot in the wood of the table. "I guess I understand why some students would stop going to class and have fun in Saltwick. But they—those students, that is—often teased or threatened those of us who wanted to stay in class."

Natalie leaned forward and covered McKenna's hand with her own. "Did anyone hurt you, sweeting?"

"N-no. A group of boys and girls cornered me in the hall on the way to class once. They called me some pretty horrible things and got awful close to me but luckily a professor made them stop."

"Healer Edmundson?"

"No, he mainly stayed in the hospital. He really didn't seem to have patience for the school when I saw him. It was Healer Misaki, the librarian. She's shorter than I am, but that day I decided I'd never cross her, Headmistress."

Natalie grinned. "You're wiser than I was at your age, McKenna. I snuck food into the library once," McKenna slapped a palm over her mouth. "Healer Misaki found out, and I was quite certain my very life was in danger."

"Someone should tell her to come back. Healer Edmundson didn't take kindly to her way of maintaining discipline and she went home."

Natalie's fingers curled into fists, fingernails digging into her palms. While she'd been lying in bed in Whitestrand, and then trying to rescue the queen in Roseharbor, good students and teachers had needed her here. "I will send a rider for her with my apologies and a personal invitation back. Hopefully, our hard work here will be a lovely surprise for her."

A corner of McKenna's mouth turned up tentatively. "I think it will. And I can't wait to work on the greenhouse."

Natalie beamed. "Neither can I. We should—

McKenna?" Natalie scrambled around the table; McKenna, her face now sickly pale, swayed alarmingly in her chair.

"Headmish ... think ... don't feel so good."

With this pronouncement, she vomited on Natalie.

CHAPTER 11

"She has a fever,"
"And a rash on her arms and torso."
"With vomiting and what you saw when you Named her, that's got to be—"

"—Kestrel fever," Natalie finished.

"The fever's here early this season," Healer Bishop observed as she and Natalie rushed to wash their hands. "I don't ever remember it striking before midwinter, but I suppose the fever had other ideas this year. We best get ready now." She handed Natalie a kerchief to tie around her nose and mouth.

Natalie rarely worked with Healer Bishop, but she was already one of Natalie's favorite members of the staff. A tall, strong woman with short, dark hair and deep brown skin, Natalie appreciated her blunt honesty and efficiency.

She gazed at McKenna, her round face a sickly pale against the white hospital linens. *At least kestrel fever comes annually and I know how it spreads. If we're all careful, we'll only have a few cases.*

"You're right. If McKenna has it, then the other students are at risk. Which means the staff will soon follow and the residents of Saltwick. I need to send word out to the Healers stationed throughout Ismereld."

"I'll get someone to tend to McKenna so I can begin handing out kerchiefs and telling people to wash their hands. Go spread the word across the Isles."

"Thank you, Healer Bishop."

"Call me Summer,"

"Thank you, Summer. Keep me posted."

At the questioning glances from students and staff on the way to her office, she simply responded: "Kestrel fever. Wash your hands and cover your faces."

People hastened to follow her instructions though Natalie didn't attribute that to her commanding presence. Ismereld had seen enough winters—and now a fall—of kestrel fever that its citizens knew to follow protocol or chance getting the disease themselves.

An hour later, she handed the first batch of letters off to a rider who would take the missives to her assigned towns.

Natalie massaged her hand, cramped as it was from writing so many copies of the letters to Healers across Ismereld. She pressed her hands to the small of her back and arched over her hands, tilting her head this way and that. Her muscles protested being bent over her desk for so long while her neck popped its relief at moving once more.

The candles in her office had burned down to stubs before she signed the last of the letters and handed them to the last rider.

Blowing out the lights in her office, Natalie shuffled to the room she shared with Jules. *Just one foot … in front of the other … keep going. Just keep going. Made it.*

She grasped the door handle when she reached the door to their room and whimpered when the handle turned in place, refusing to open the door. Natalie pounded on the door. "Jules? Let me in, the doorknob finally broke."

He's probably with a patient. This doorknob has been loose since we returned. Why didn't I have someone come fix it? I'm so tired; I just want to get in bed.

No one came.

Natalie turned and fell against the door, her back sliding against the wood as she slid down to the floor, face in her palms.

"Nat, are you all right?"

Natalie lifted one eyelid. A pale concerned face hung in the dim corridor like the full moon in the night sky. "Oh, hey, Em. What are you doing here? I, um, can't get into my room. The doorknob broke."

"I was on my way to see a patient and I found you. I'll go get someone to fix the door. Will you be okay until I get back?"

Natalie flapped a hand, letting the one eyelid she'd opened drift closed. "Sure."

I am the Headmistress. I shouldn't be seen like this. People will see I'm weak. They'll think I can't do this.

Natalie clambered to her feet, wobbly as a newborn fawn, and leaned her back against the stone wall opposite her door. Putting her palms against the stone behind her, she dug her fingertips into the rough surface in an effort to stay focused and present, not to mention awake.

Em returned and the person she brought, bless them, installed a new doorknob. As Em helped her to bed, a jolt of panic lanced though her chest. "Em, did I thank whoever fixed our door?"

Em tugged off one of Natalie's boots and then the other. "You did, don't worry."

"Who came to help?"

"Healer Boseman. She fixed a lot of the tools and hardware on her family's farm before coming here."

"I should ... I should know these things," Natalie nestled her head into her pillow, tears escaping the corners of her eyes.

"You're still getting on your feet as Headmistress. You'll get there."

"I thought I was, but now kestrel fever has come early, and—"

"Kestrel fever comes every year and people will be fine as long as they follow the protocols. Even McKenna will probably recover since we caught it early enough."

Natalie blew out a breath closed her eyes. "Goddess, what a mess."

"It's not your fault, Nat."

"I suppose not."

"Nat, it's not your fault."

"I know," Natalie snapped. "I'm sorry, I didn't mean to take that tone of voice. I just … Em, I used to be able to do so many things. You and I, we used to stay awake until all hours studying. And I might've been tired the next day, but it was … well, it was possible without ill effects. Now, I can't seem to do anything without making myself exhausted or setting my headaches off. Most of the students respect me, but a lot of the staff don't. And now this fever. Everything's falling apart." Natalie knuckled a tear off her cheek.

Em wiped another tear off Natalie's face with her thumb. "You're doing the best you can with what you have. No one could ask for more than that."

"I know. The thing is … what if my best isn't enough?"

It would be one thing if I felt rested after a good night's sleep. But I don't.

Natalie strode through the Abbey hallways the next morning with Jake. She praised students for wearing their kerchiefs and washing their hands at the extra hand-washing stations Healer Bishop had set up. Her body moved quickly but her brain felt slow and foggy. Even a strong cup of tea at breakfast did little to help her feel more alert.

What else did Gayla do during kestrel fever season besides have everyone cover their noses and mouths and wash their hands a lot?

I don't know; I don't remember. Maybe it's in a library book or one of Gayla's journals or…

I don't have time for that! What makes the most sense to do?

Taking action silenced the argumentative voices in her head. She strode to the barn, ignoring Bonnie the stable master's protests as she tacked a shining bay gelding herself, swung her leg over his back and trotted toward Saltwick.

Entering Saltwick, she steered her horse straight to the Town Hall, requested and was granted an immediate meeting with Magistrate Levi.

Being Headmistress had its privileges.

Entering the magistrate's office, a tall man with dark hair, rosy cheeks and a wide smile greeted Natalie warmly. "Headmistress Desmond, I'm so pleased to meet you. The hero of Desmond's Fever has come home and is now Headmistress. I think it's fitting, don't you?"

Natalie forced the smile to stay on her face. "Yes."

"What brings you to see me today?"

"Kestrel fever."

"This early?"

"Yes. We need to be sure everyone in town takes preventative measures." Natalie detailed everything the town's residents must do to keep the outbreak to a minimum. "If anyone shows any signs at all, such as vomiting, fever or a rash on their upper body, send them to us right away. In fact, I'm going to have two Healers come stay in town, just in case."

"No problem."

They arranged where they Healers would obtain food and lodging.

Natalie stood to leave. "Thank you for your assistance, Magistrate Levi. I'm glad there's someone in Saltwick who knows the importance of keeping this year's outbreak in check."

"No problem. I'm so glad Headmistress Gayla has such an excellent, if young, successor. Oh, by the way, I heard you suffer from terrible headaches, is that true?"

Natalie twisted the end of her braid. "Um, yes. Sometimes, yes."

"My wife used to have the worst headaches. The Abbey tried so many things, but they went away when she got pregnant. Have you thought about having a baby?"

Clutching her hands so they didn't shake—or hit the man—Natalie whirled and threw open the door to the magistrate's office. Cloak billowing behind her, she made her way back to her horse, mounted and trotted out of town. When Saltwick was out of sight, she urged her horse to a canter and then let him have his head.

The biting wind eroded the pounding in her ears and the rushing blood inside her veins. With each stride her horse took, the tumult in her head settled like so much silt in a river.

Back at the Abbey, Natalie made a bee line for the hospital, this time carrying the black leather-bound book she'd purchased in Ebenos Point Keep to jot down her notes as Charlotte's Healing teacher.

"Healer Bishop," she greeted the other woman upon entering the hospital. "Any new kestrel fever cases?"

Natalie snatched up the nearest quill and jotted Healer Bishop's updates in her book. There was only one new infection, thank the Five, and the Healers on duty had quarantined the new patient and McKenna in a corner of the hospital. She glanced over and nodded approvingly at the curtained-off area.

"Excellent. Don't hesitate to use the quarantine rooms if need be."

"We won't. Since we have only two patients, it's manageable here in the main hospital room. Considering the quarantine rooms don't have windows, I'd rather keep working by candlelight to a minimum."

"Putting other patients at risk for infection for the sake of having more light is unacceptable," Healer Edmundson put in.

Natalie grit her teeth. *Obviously, he wants to find out just how cranky I get from fatigue, pain, near-constant harassment and strangers asking me if I've tried getting pregnant to fix my bloody headaches.*

"The patients are fine."

"The kestrel fever ones, yes. But keeping them in here is a risk to all the other patients."

Several of her staff muttered their dissent. Natalie lowered her voice to a near-whisper. "Keep your voice down, Healer. There is no need to cause panic. Keeping patients in the main hospital room is only a danger if they touch, vomit or sneeze on others or if their Healers fail to be cautious. The other Healers here seem capable of preventing contamination between areas. I trust you are, too."

For the second time that day, Natalie turned on her heel and left.

CHAPTER 12

"We've been here more than a month. It's time to find out what Ystrelle's been up to," Anli said one morning, nearly giddy with the prospect.

Onlo nodded his agreement. "Hopefully Charlotte is still being held in the same room. Maybe we can get her out this time."

"It makes me nervous that we've been here so long and haven't heard a thing. She has to know I'm here. Why hasn't she come for me and forced me to marry Charlotte?" Jules put in. "I would think she'd be at least as determined to marry me off as my mother."

The same thought had been lurking at the edge of Natalie's thoughts. "Anli, why don't you go back to Roseharbor and she—see what she knows. Get Charlotte out only if it's safe."

"With respect Natalie, I would like to be the one to go." Onlo interjected.

Natalie met Onlo's gaze. It wasn't imploring; he wasn't

begging her. But one look into his eyes and she was transported back to the corridor in Ebenos Point Keep where she'd secretly witnessed Charlotte and Onlo gazing at each other. The depth of their feelings had shaken her to her core. And she knew all too well what it was like when someone you loved had been kidnapped. Guilt flooded through her when she realized how long she'd kept Onlo at the Abbey.

"You're right, you should be the one to go. Leave as soon as you're ready."

Onlo stood from the table heading swiftly for the door. "I will send word as soon as I can."

Anli made to follow him. "I need to help him plan the palace break in."

Natalie fixed her with a stare. "And after he leaves, I need you to take over his self-defense and outdoor survival classes."

Anli blinked, dark eyebrows rising. "Seriously Natalie? You want *me* teaching people? How well do you think that will go?"

Jules pressed a hand over his mouth to stifle his laughter. Natalie glared at him and turned her gaze to Anli. "As well as you make it go."

Anli's eyes narrowed. "A lot of them aren't going to like me. You know how I am."

Natalie shrugged. "A lot of them don't like me. You'll be fine, Professor Yun."

Onlo left that afternoon at which time several more knots took up residence in Natalie's stomach. Her sleep, already disrupted by Jules's occasional nightmares and calls from the hospital, became even worse. She forced herself through each day, her ability to think muddier than ever. To top it all off, her speech got worse.

Once, when she was a child, a traveling band of performers from Methyseld Isle came to her hometown of

Mistfell. She remembered holding her breath as the acrobats flew twisting through the air with nothing but the ground beneath them. *Making new decisions every day, hurdling headfirst into running the Abbey. I'm just like one of those acrobats—one slip and I'll plummet to the ground and this will all be over.*

In an effort to combat her anxiety, Natalie made a point to visit all aspects of the Abbey daily, journal in hand. Even when the fatigue threatened to drag her into the ground or her head pounded like a hammer on an anvil, she simply couldn't rest until she confirmed everything was running smoothly. On days she struggled with her health, the rough, aged stone walls supported her as Jake inspected operations in her stead.

The hospital is back to its usual number of patients, thank The Five. The Kestrel fever patients had all recovered. The hospital also no longer had a constant influx of war wounded that it had the past spring. Apparently Ystrelle, in all her benevolence, allowed Charlotte to negotiate peace with Lorelan, the country across Bridhe's Channel from Ismereld.

Classes ran smoothly once more, and the greenhouse and the drying room next to it were restored to pristine conditions. Natalie longed to teach a class of her own, but it simply wasn't possible. Every day she sat in her office for hours poring over paperwork until her head was splitting and she had to go take a nap.

"Gayla never needed to nap; she handled this workload with ease, even at an advanced age. But I can't do it; if I don't take a nap, then by dinnertime I can't even function," Natalie tearfully confided to Em over lunch one day. She couldn't stomach the idea of confessing such things to Jules and adding to the guilt he already felt.

"Is there anyone on the staff you trust to Heal you? I could try, you know I would, but head injuries are not something I have experience with." Em offered.

"I know. Thank you. There is someone I'd like to consult. But I'm terrified of un-um-undermining what little respect I've earned. It's been really hard getting the staff to view me as their Headmistress. And some still have major issues with me. If I go to a professor as a patient, how would that look?" Natalie dabbed her eyes with her sleeve. "Word of my condition spread like wildfire; one patient in the hospital the other day even knew about it. She even told me I should eat a raw potato until my headache goes away."

Em nearly spit out her drink. "A potato?"

"A potato. A raw one," Natalie giggled pressing her palms to her forehead.

Em's eyes rolled skyward. "And to think the cure was in the root cellar all along."

Natalie shook her head. "I know. Even worse, the magistrate in Saltwick said I should get pregnant to cure my headaches."

Em held a napkin to her alarmingly scarlet face in a desperate attempt to keep in her mouthful of soup.

"Don't choke," Natalie scolded, holding her stomach as she doubled over with mirth. "Unfortunately, potatoes and babies notwithstanding, I need to get back to work."

Natalie walked from the Great Hall to her office nodding and saying hello to students and staff alike, one of the many knots in her stomach twinging when she wondered whether her foggy brain got their names right. Upon entering her office, she spied the stack of paperwork on her desk, turned and walked back out.

A familiar cacophony greeted Natalie as she entered the warmth of the Abbey's animal sanctuary. The short, stout form of Healer Euphemia Bowers bent over an injured black cat with rather large ears, who, as a testament to Healer Bowers's skills, submitted to the treatment quietly.

"What do you want?" Healer Bowers demanded.

Natalie's jaw dropped when Healer Bowers, upon seeing who had entered, stopped treating her feline patient entirely.

"I'll not have you meddling here, Healer Desmond. That

young upstart Edmundson came in a few months ago and I kicked him right out on his bum. You'll go the same way if you try to take over my animals."

Natalie held up a hand, hoping to calm both Healer Bowers, and the cat, whose yellow-green eyes had turned to her, tail now swishing back and forth. "Actually, I'm here because I need your help."

Healer Bowers returned her attentions to the cat. "Is Jake all right? I don't see him with you."

"He's fine. I-it's-well, *I* need your help. I need you to try to Heal me."

Healer Bowers dropped her palms to either side of the cat who glared at Natalie.

"Do you see any humans here Healer Desmond? This isn't the human sanctuary. It's the animal one. I don't get along with humans overmuch. That's why I'm here."

"I figured. I'm here because I feel you're the only one I can trust. I have a brain injury, you see." Natalie related the story of the throne room battle, how Jules touching her head to draw the last of her energy put her in a coma, and her lingering side effects.

"So you see," Natalie raised a shaking hand and dabbed tears from her eyes. I need privacy. And discretion. Two things I will find in abundance here in your sanctuary."

Healer Bowers and her feline patient regarded Natalie in stony silence.

"Fine," she said at last. "Have a seat." She indicated a chair near her examination table, in which Natalie obediently took a seat. Healer Bowers scooped up the cat and placed it in Natalie's lap. "Hold this fellow while I Name you."

Natalie stroked the midnight-black fur, and the cat pinned its ears back and nipped Natalie's hand.

Healer Bowers squatted in front of her cranky patient. "She's a friend."

The cat trilled and butted its head against Natalie's chest. Natalie gawked at the cat. *Did ... did he just understand what she said?*

Healer Bowers put her hands on Natalie's shoulders. "All right, both of you be still."

Natalie's stomach roiled. *What if she finds something terrible? What if she finds nothing? What if…*

The black cat rolled over on her lap, purring loudly, and she put a hand on its reddish-brown belly and breathed.

Healer Bowers let out a breath. "Well, like I said, I'm no expert. But I can see the awful inflammation in your head, neck and shoulders. Your head trauma is unlike any I've ever seen. I don't know that we can fix it, but managing the symptoms might be possible."

"I've tried dullanbark tea. It doesn't help. I might as well drink water."

"Well, I know what I'd recommend for animals. Let me check in the library to see if it's safe for humans to use. There are a few other things I'll research there as well. I can't promise any results, though."

Natalie rose. "I understand. Thank you. Both for your time and your discretion." She reluctantly handed the cat back. "With those ears and that coat, he looks like a bat."

Healer Bowers cradled her patient like a baby and kissed his head. "He does."

"I hope he gets better soon." Natalie called from the door.

"He will. And we might just find something to help you yet, Headmistress."

CHAPTER 13

"**D**o you think we should teach offensive magery?" Jules asked Natalie.

Natalie clasped her gloved hand in his as they hiked through the frosty woods with Jake one week after Onlo's departure.

"I don't know," Natalie considered this for a moment. She'd been the one to encourage Jules to use his mage powers as a weapon. It had been their only way to survive the battle after Ystrelle captured them and brought them to Roseharbor Palace. Even so, the thought of teaching new mages to attack using their newfound powers disturbed her.

"This may sound hypocritical of me, but I just can't find it in my heart to think that it's a eye-a-g-good idea," Natalie admitted. "The circumstances in which you used your powers to attack were unique. Frankly, I'd rather people use Onlo and Anli's self-defense techniques if they need to get themselves out of a tough situation."

Jules stepped over a tree root, nodding. "I agree with you. Especially since we've begun to teach students how to

Heal with partners. I don't want the Healer mages to find out they can use a partner as a source of energy." His Adam's apple bobbed up and down "I don't want anyone dying because someone gets too power-hungry."

Healers working in pairs was something rather unheard of at the Abbey. Until now, the Abbey curriculum required Healers to Heal on their own. As a young Healing student, this had made sense to Natalie. Since there were so many more patients than Healers, the ability to Heal on one's own was a necessity, whether it be in small towns or in the Abbey's hospital.

Natalie had never questioned tradition until Jules lost his hand and, as a result, could no longer Name patients properly. It had been a shot in the dark, but Natalie's idea of combining her energies with his paid off.

Deciding she had enough with tradition, Natalie had added Healing in pairs to the curriculum. After all, she figured, we must prepare Healers for any eventuality. Plus, it kept Healing accessible to people whose bodies made it difficult to perform the task alone.

This made her the subject of whispers from the staff yet again. She shrugged under her winter cloak. *Just another day as Headmistress.*

Whispers behind her back were, Natalie discovered, rather like weeds in a garden. They were everywhere and sprouted up every time she turned around. Once, she came upon two professors gossiping about her in the hallway. When they spotted her, they turned and continued their conversation a nearby classroom.

Marching to the door, Natalie crossed her arms and pinned both of them with a glare. "If talking about me in the hall is too embarrassing, why were you out here in the first place? And for Five's sake, haven't you ever heard of closing the damned door?" Emerald cloak whirling behind her, she turned and stalked away.

She had known when she became Headmistress that she would need to assert her power and authority; she just hadn't known it would take so long for people to come around.

Returning home from her hike with Jules, Natalie beheld an entourage of beautiful horses and a carriage pulling up in front of the Abbey. Her heart leaped. *Has Onlo rescued Charlotte? Is she here?*

Sharing a hopeful glance with Jules, they ran hand in hand to the Abbey entrance.

The excitement running through Natalie's veins fizzled and died when Head Councilwoman Geeta Ramesh alighted from the carriage stairs.

She forced a smile on her face. "Head Councilwoman, how lovely to see you."

"Headmistress," the Head Councilwoman greeted her. "I've come to check on your progress here at the Abbey."

The knots in Natalie's stomach drew so tight a wave of nausea washed over her. She gestured inside the Abbey front door. "Right this way."

Natalie showed the Head Councilwoman the restored library, students hard at work in their classes, the hospital, and the pristine greenhouse. Once back in her office, Natalie spoke about the changes she'd made to the curriculum already and several more she had in mind. The Head Councilwoman nodded in approval; Natalie let out a breath she didn't realize she'd been holding.

"And what do your staff think of all these changes?" the Head Councilwoman said accepting a cup of tea from Natalie.

Natalie poured her own cup of tea and gratefully wrapped her fingers around the delicate, warm cup.

The tea set was one she'd purchased in Saltwick from a visiting Attuned citizen of Citherin. The thin, dark green porcelain painted with elegant sprays of white flowers had called to Natalie immediately.

"Many have been flexible with the changes," Natalie hedged, taking a sip and weighing her next words.

The Head Councilwoman smirked. "And many, no

doubt, challenge you both openly and behind closed doors, yes?"

Natalie swallowed her tea and pursed her lips. "Most times just right to my face."

"People do not like change, especially here in the Isles. We are steeped in our traditions. Many assume 'the way it used to be' must be better by default. It's one of the reasons I want you here shaking things up."

Yes, but at what cost? I hardly sleep. My headaches are terrible and my health is getting worse.

Not wanting the Head Councilwoman to see her misgivings she nodded

"You don't believe me?"

"No, I do—I mean you're right about people and I thank you for your compliments. It's just—I'm still not sure I'm the right person for this job."

"Hm. What I actually hear you saying is 'what if all the people whispering about me are correct?' That you're too young, you don't know what you're doing and that your brain is too injured to do the job."

Natalie's eyes flashed to the Head Councilwoman over her tea. She swallowed painfully. "Yes."

The Head Councilwoman placed her cup in its matching saucer on the desk, leaned forward, put her elbows on the desk and interlaced her fingers. "The more important question is what do *you* believe? Do *you* believe you're the person for this job? There will always be others who doubt you. I have people who doubt me. But, if *you* believe in yourself, then you are indeed the right person to be Headmistress."

Natalie tried to blink back tears and failed. How often had she sat in this office—right where the Head Councilwoman sat now—and received guidance and wisdom from Headmistress Gayla? Over a cup of tea. Now, once again she received a much needed message, but this time, she was on the other side of the desk.

"I can understand that it might take some time for that

to sink in. Even more for you to truly believe it. But, judging from how improved things are around here, you've at least done a good job of pretending."

A small laugh escaped Natalie despite her tears.

"I must go now," the Head Councilwoman stood. "I need to face—"

A frantic knock sounded on Natalie's office door.

"Come in," Natalie answered.

A young student darted in, entirely out of breath. "Headmistress, a rider just arrived, come quickly."

Natalie dashed out from behind her desk and ran towards the Abbey entrance. *By the Five, please be Onlo this time.*

Bursting out the front door, she blinked several times at the rider atop a tall chestnut horse. The bright sun glinted off a cascade of silver hair pouring over elegant clothes.

"Charlotte!"

CHAPTER 14

"She took Onlo," Charlotte whispered and slid sideways off her horse. Natalie threw her arms around her queen, stumbling backward in an effort to keep them both from falling to the ground.

"Get a stretcher! We need to get this woman to the hospital," she shouted.

The muscles in her arms screaming as she kneeled down, Natalie adjusted the queen so Charlotte's back was against her chest. She placed her hands on Charlotte's shoulders and closed her eyes. Heart pounding against her ribcage, she reached into Ismereld and allowed the Isle's magic to flow through her and into Charlotte. The magic answered; in her mind, Natalie could see the queen's body and all its systems outlined in blue.

Her eyes fluttered open. "She's exhausted but I can't find anything physically wrong," she said to no one in particular.

Four Healers came bustling out of the Abbey door with a stretcher, green cloaks swirling in the fall wind. They placed the stretcher next to the queen and Natalie helped transfer the unconscious girl onto the stretcher, intensely aware that the Head Councilwoman of the Isles watched from several feet away.

Natalie escorted the team of people carrying the queen back to the hospital, stomach roiling and fists clenched. *Hell in a kettle, we got Charlotte back but now we've lost Onlo to Ystrelle.* She bit her lip to keep a string of very un-Headmistress-like curses inside.

Once back in the hospital, Natalie sent one of the Abbey's ubiquitous messengers for Jules, Anli and Em. Pulling up a chair next to Charlotte's bedside, Natalie fell into it, head falling into her palms, the fatigue and grief threatening to pull her under.

She looked up when a warm hand clasped her shoulder. She clasped Jules's hand and reported what she found during her Naming.

Jules Named Charlotte himself, and then raised his eyes to meet Natalie's. "I sense the same thing."

Natalie nodded, twirling her braid around in one of her hands. When Jules had become a fully trained mage, he no longer needed her energy to Heal—and he could Heal on any Isle. It was hard to swallow at first, but today she was grateful to have someone she trusted so much by her side in a situation such as this.

Natalie leaned closer to Jules. "Her wounds. They're not physical."

Jules swallowed. "No. No, they're not."

"Where am I?"

Natalie lifted her head and grasped her friend's hand. "Here at the Abbey, sweeting. You got away, you're safe."

Charlotte blinked a few times. A tear trickled down her cheek making her look less like a queen and more like the scared young woman she was.

"I want to go back to sleep, let me go back to sleep. I

saw my parents. In my dreams. They asked me to forgive them and … and I did. I asked them to forgive *me* but … but I don't know …"

"Hush, there's nothing to forgive. You did nothing wrong. It's not your fault Ystrelle captured Onlo."

The princess wrenched her hand from Natalie's grasp, pressing her hands against her eyes. "No, no you don't understand. They never understand."

"I don't know how to fix this," Natalie whispered to Jules.

Jules clasped Charlotte's other hand. "Can you help us understand? Tell us what happened to you. I know what it's like to be held captive. You can tell me anything."

Charlotte shook her head violently. "No, no I can't. I can't tell you. They can't make me."

Natalie and Jules shared a glance. "Then just start at the beginning," Jules suggested. "Do you know why she sent you back and kept Onlo?"

The queen yanked her hands from Natalie's and Jules's and covered her mouth as if she might keep in the unspeakable horrors. Eyes wide as saucers, she slid her palms to her cheeks. "She's holding him hostage. She knows how much I love him and what his death would do to me. She sent me here to get you," she turned her head to look at Jules. "You're to return to Roseharbor Palace with me. Natalie, too. Natalie would be your hostage. That's what she does, you see."

Natalie rubbed her neck in a vain attempt to ease the ominous ache growing under her fingertips. "She's going after those of us who were on Solerin this past summer? And holding that person's loved one hostage?"

The queen's face crumpled "Not us. Not us who visited Solerin. Mages. Any mage she can find. She's been searching for them. Aldworth didn't find enough for her so she's been looking for them herself. The palace is now full of mages—plus one family member for each mage. The person who will die if the mage does not comply."

Natalie swallowed the bile in her throat.

"We need to tell the Special Ops guild to step it up finding mages; they need to know what they're up against," Jules said in a dead voice.

"That's not the worst of it," Charlotte whispered.

Natalie stroked the side of her face. "What is it darling? You can tell us."

The queen closed her eyes and pressed her hands to her head, shaking it back and forth fighting off demons only she could see. "Ystrelle has a munitions expert. Someone from Obfuselt she captured several years ago. His team was sent to Solerin on a mission and it went wrong. Ystrelle kept him and he's been developing Obfuselt weapons technology for her." Her eyes flew open, the whites showing as she glanced back and forth between them. "That's how they were able to blow us out of the water last summer. This man put Obfuselt technology on the boat that sank us."

Anli swore. Natalie turned to the foot of the bed; Em and Anli stood hand in hand, faces pale. "I want to find that man and find out why he assisted Ystrelle. Even if he was captured and tortured, that's no excuse for what he did."

"Well, you might have that opportunity soon," Charlotte choked finally breaking down in sobs "Whether Jules or Natalie come back with me or not, Ystrelle is on her way with mages and explosives. She's going to destroy the Abbey."

CHAPTER 15

Silence rang in Natalie's ears.

"When will she be here?"

"How did you find this out when you were stuck in that room?"

"How much time do we have?"

"Everyone be quiet," Natalie ordered when Charlotte curled up into a ball clutching her head with her hands. Placing a comforting hand on Charlotte, she turned to her friends. "What will we do? We have no defenses. Historically, the Queensguard has defended us in times of need. But Ystrelle controls the Queensguard."

The Head Councilwoman stepped forward. "I will call an emergency meeting of the people I trust most. I will send all the help I can."

Natalie barely remembered her manners in time. "Thank you, Head Councilwoman," she managed before the other woman swept from the hospital.

"Will the walls be enough to keep her out? They've stood two thousand years."

Anli rolled her eyes. "Don't be dense, Headmistress," she used the term sarcastically. "They have one of my own with them—or at least he used to be. It might take a while, but these walls will fall."

Natalie grasped Jules's hand across Charlotte and exchanged a desperate glance with him. "What can we do? What should I do? I've barely gotten on my feet as Headmistress. We just put this place back together."

"We evacuate," Jules stated flatly.

"But to where? Where can we house all the students and staff? Where is there room for the hospital and animal sanctuary? And damned if I'm leaving without the library."

"I have an idea," Charlotte's muffled voice surprised them all. She uncurled from her fetal position and moved to a sitting position. Natalie's heart sunk at her red-rimmed eyes and strands of hair hanging dull and scraggly around her face.

"During the epidemic, when my family fled Roseharbor, we tried to go to a hotel we used to stay at when I was a child. But since we traveled in secret, we could not send word ahead. We got there, and the hotel was abandoned. It's very large; it's one of the reasons my parents picked it when they evacuated the palace."

The old hotel sat by Lake Clanairys up in the mountains, roughly three hours away by horseback west of the Abbey. Charlotte answered everyone's questions about the facility. Listening to Charlotte's descriptions, Natalie got the sense that it just might work.

I'd really have to see it before I declare it a temporary home for my Abbey. But how much time do we have before Ystrelle strikes?

"Charlotte can you tell me how you learned of this attack when you were in the palace?"

"That's the thing," Charlotte looked pleadingly at Natalie. "I don't know if this is information I got by accident or they let it slip on purpose. I don't know if Ystrelle knows I know. Do you know what I mean? I'm terrified that she wanted me to know and now I'm playing into her hands by telling you." Charlotte covered her face again crumbling. "I'm not making any sense; I can't seem to make any sense."

"Just tell me how you discovered the information," Natalie said soothingly.

"I heard two people discussing an attack on the Abbey in the hallway outside my room. It was nighttime. I think they thought I was asleep."

"What precisely did they say?" Anli demanded

"I don't remember their exact words, but they said there were enough explosives in one of the palace outbuildings to take down a city. The other guard asked what they were for. The first guard told her Ystrelle was going after the Abbey."

Natalie blanched. "'Enough to take down a city'. By the Five, I hope they were exaggerating."

"I doubt it," Em said quietly. "This is Ystrelle we're talking about."

Natalie stood and strode to one of the hospital windows. Trees swayed in the fall winds, brown, red and yellow leaves skittering over the Abbey grounds. The wind chased leaves up the walls and in swirls.

Should I order everyone to leave this beloved place based solely on some whispers Charlotte heard outside her door? And why did Ystrelle let Charlotte go? Why give up her very own personal puppet queen? I don't like it. At all.

A chill swept down Natalie's spine and she wrenched her braid until her scalp hurt. Ystrelle's actions made no sense. Her unpredictable behavior made her a danger to the Abbey and everyone within its walls. Which left one logical choice before her.

Natalie strode back over to her queen's bedside. "We evacuate."

Natalie set a goal of evacuating the entire Abbey in five days. It had never done to her knowledge. *Another thing I'll make up as I go. By the Five, I hope we get out in time.*

She, Jules, Anli and Em stayed up late that night

planning the logistics of the evacuation. Jake dozed on the cushion Natalie had put next to her desk just for him.

The candles in Natalie's office had nearly guttered out when Anli suggested a small group of people stay behind. "We can create the illusion we still occupy the Abbey. What Ystrelle will find instead is booby traps and foes who disappear as soon as they attack."

Jules grinned wickedly at her across Natalie's desk. "I like it."

Natalie rested her elbows on the arms of her chair and steepled her fingers. "Brilliant."

"We'll do it together," Em said, squeezing Anli's hand.

"You are evacuating with the rest of the staff." Anli's tone brooked no argument.

"I am staying with you and I am protecting my home. I love you, but you cannot tell me where to go and what to do," Em retorted.

"I can if you're endangering your life."

Em stood, glaring daggers at her partner. "You're risking your life; why can't I risk mine?"

Anli rose, her face close to Em's. "Because I trained for combat my whole life. This is not childbirth, love. This is *war*."

Unnerved by the shouting. Jake slinked over and pressed his side against Natalie's leg. Placing a reassuring hand on his head, Natalie exchanged an uncomfortable glance with Jules. Averting her eyes from the argument, she suppressed a hysterical giggle at the people walking by her office staring, the heated exchange between the two women impossible to ignore.

Natalie stepped gingerly around her desk and grasped Jules's hand intending to leave the two women to it. But before they could move, both women stomped out, going separate ways.

Natalie swallowed. "Well, that was … fun."

Jules blew out a breath, scrubbing his face with his palm. "Let's go to bed."

Taking Jules's hand, Natalie followed him to their quarters, Jake padding in their wake. It was all she could do to summon the energy to take off her boots and cloak before snuggling up against Jules and falling asleep.

Natalie gave the order to evacuate the next morning, and the Abbey bustled like a hive of bees.

Students and professors, once they packed up their own belongings, helped pack the library books into rough-hewn crates. The Healers treated many strained back muscles the day everyone loaded the crates into carts borrowed from local farmers.

The carts left as soon as the library was empty. Their destination was a farm located on the way to Lake Clanairys. When the Abbey evacuated, they'd stop at the farm and pick up the carts and with them, Healer Misaki, who had accepted Natalie's invitation to return and whom Natalie trusted to watch over the library's contents implicitly.

There was a stony silence between Em and Anli as they each fulfilled their tasks preparing for the leave taking.

Anli avoided the situation by simply taking to the woods with her students and setting as many traps as she could for Ystrelle's forces.

In the midst of all the chaos, Charlotte's condition improved such that she was able to take food and begin walking around. She even helped with light work. Nonetheless, Natalie worried about her. She refused to talk about her experiences during captivity, even to Jules who'd been a prisoner twice himself. As she and Jake oversaw the evacuation, Natalie often spotted Charlotte laying down, eyes wide and empty. *I must try to Heal her again once the we leave. I'll ask every single member about mental trauma if I have to. But I'm going to help her.*

Natalie doled out the decisions from the late night meetings with her friends and Healer Edmundson harassed her about every single one. From the decision to evacuate to what day they would leave, everything was fair game for his criticism. Two days after preparations began, Natalie finally snapped. "Look, stay here and die if you wish. As for myself, I am going to ensure the safety of the students, staff, the books and the hospital. Now get out of my way."

Natalie and Jules walked through the empty halls of the Abbey holding hands, Jake beside them, tail down. The ghosts of two thousand years of teachers and students haunted the classrooms. Their footsteps echoed through the dark, cavernous library; neither of them could stand to stay very long.

The evening shift of Healers prepared the hospital's patients for travel. The contents of the stockroom now sat in a wagon outside the hospital.

"One more place to go," Jules whispered.

They walked reverently to the cloisters and crossed the frosty grass to the greenhouse. Wordlessly, Natalie followed Jules inside, running her fingertips along the well-worn work table at which she'd spent so many happy hours.

Jules put his arms around her from behind and rested his chin on her shoulder. "When I first came back to the Abbey this past spring, I saw you for the first time right there in the greenhouse doorway."

Natalie smiled at the memory. "I couldn't believe you'd finally come back. You looked like you did in every one of my dreams."

Jules kissed her neck. "I couldn't believe my former student had grown into a beautiful woman."

Natalie arched her neck like a cat to encourage further kisses even as heat flooded her cheeks at the compliment.

"I was so—" Jules said in between his attentions to her, "—conflicted."

A corner of Natalie's mouth turned up wryly. "I could tell. We fought several times that very day."

He tickled her for her cheekiness. Natalie shrieked and

ran away, but he caught her around the waist in the drying room and pinned her to the wall with his forearms. "You know what I meant."

"I know what you meant," she parroted, tilting her chin up and nipping his ear. "I had to flat out tell you that I was eighteen and no longer a forbidden, off-limits student before you would even kiss me."

Jules ran his thumb over her cheek. "Thank Goddess you did." His mouth descended to hers, sending frissons of heat all the way to Natalie's toes. Hearing a moan she belatedly identified as her own, she threaded her fingers through his dark hair and pulled him closer, pressing her body against his. But she couldn't ever seem to get close enough. Would that she could disappear inside him and they would become one person.

Sighing sweetly into her mouth, Jules broke the kiss and leaned his forehead against hers. "We have someplace to be."

She nodded reluctantly, clasping his hand in one of her own.

It was time to say goodbye to her Abbey

.

CHAPTER 16

With the most important of their worldly possessions on their back, the students waited in front of the Abbey. Trading glances and uncharacteristically silent, relief washed over their faces when they spotted Natalie. Even the snarl of knots in her stomach couldn't dampen the surge of confidence this gave her.

Mounting her horse, Natalie slung her own brown leather satchel of herbs and supplies over her head and onto her shoulder. She sat astride a towering, dark bay horse with two white stockings named Arthur. Sitting upon such a majestic mount, her shoulders dropped down and back and her spine stretched taller as she rode around the perimeter of the crowd.

She smiled and nodded to her staff as they helped organize and comfort the students, their own belongings strapped to their backs.

Satisfied the group was ready to go, she turned Arthur toward the road and directed him to stand beside Jules and his mount, Elric. He sent up sparks from his hand; the signal for everyone to fall in line behind him.

Natalie reined Arthur over to the side of the road and made sure people followed Jules. As children and teachers passed in front of her, the crisp fall wind blowing her hair out from under her hood, she took one last glance at the Abbey entrance. The stone walls rose protectively out of the darkness and warm lights glowed in the windows, the work of Anli's team making sure the Abbey still appeared fully occupied. *Please Goddess, let this be temporary. Keep everyone safe until we return. I know the Abbey is more than just a building. It's all of us. But please, please keep it safe while we're gone.*

Turning Arthur in a circle as the end of the line walked by, she cast her mind about for anything she might have forgotten to take care of. The increasing ache in her head had no response.

By the Five, I just want to keep us all safe from Ystrelle. Give me the strength to do that, please.

Halfway to Lake Clanairys, one of the carriages meant for the hospital patients pulled up alongside Natalie. Cheeks flaming and tears pricking her eyes, she eyed the carriage longingly. The pounding headache and bone-crushing fatigue fought with her need to stay on her horse and set an example of strength for her students and staff.

Unable to stay upright any longer, she slid off Arthur, nearly collapsing under the weight of her satchel when her feet hit the ground. She offered him to the nearest staff member with a weak pat on the neck. Heaving out a breath, she climbed the stairs into the carriage, slumped onto the burgundy velvet bench seat and jumped when arms enfolded her from behind.

Jules pressed a kiss to her temple. "You are doing the right thing."

"Am I?" She sobbed. "We've abandoned our home based on some whispers Charlotte heard outside her door at Roseharbor Palace. And I can't even do my job as Headmistress because my head hurts too much and my body just won't do what it's supposed to do."

Jules rocked her gently back and forth. "Better to keep everyone safe then risk Ystrelle's wrath. And you can't take care of anyone unless you take care of yourself first."

"How long does it take, Jules?"

"For what?"

"After a severe injury. How long does it take until you stop feeling broken?"

Jules was silent for a few moments. "Please know, I still haven't given up hope that you'll get better, at least somewhat." He sighed. "But, if not, eventually you will adapt. Some days, your new normal state won't even bother you. Other days will be worse." He cradled her head against his shoulder. "Sleep, my love. We'll be there soon."

I've already given up my home and the ability to ride a horse during the evacuation. I refuse to sleep as we lead our people to safety.

The next thing she knew the sun flickered against her closed eyelids. Squinting, she spied a fir tree-lined road in the mountains.

Jules must've been aware that she was awake; she felt his arms tighten about her. Sometime after she'd fallen asleep, he'd pulled her back against his chest and piled warm furs over both of them. Warm and snug, a sense of well-being washed over her, despite everything that lay ahead. She nestled further into Jules and squeezed him back.

"We're almost there," he whispered.

"Who is leading the way?"

"Charlotte. She's the one who's been there after all."

"Mmmkay. Do you remember riding bareback on Elric earlier this spring?" Natalie closed her eyes and let the sun shine through her eyelids. "I felt so warm and content and I wanted to stay like that forever."

Jules rested his chin on her head. "You can still be with me forever. This is a dream we share, and I don't see why it can't come true."

"But Ystrelle—"

"Ystrelle has enough. Let's not give her our future, too."

Taking Jules's hand while alighting from the carriage, Natalie surveyed the old hotel. The building sprawled in between Lake Clanairys and the nearest mountain. A large, wooden barn with a giant hole in the roof sat off to its right. The white paint covering the wooden siding peeled off in curls. It had loads of windows each of which had red shutters that matched the fall leaves swirling about her feet. A veranda, painted the same color as the shutters, wrapped around the hotel and out of sight.

Aware of all the eyes on her, Natalie approached the doors and knocked loudly. Despite Charlotte's claims the place was vacant, it seemed only prudent to confirm so. When no one answered her repeated knocks, she turned the doorknob. Although locked, the rusted mechanism gave way and fell to the ground with an ominous thud.

She stepped into the foyer of the hotel, praying the creaking floor didn't give out from underneath her. A cobwebbed crystal chandelier hung overhead and a grand staircase spiraled up and out of view.

A bird, startled by Natalie's presence flew out a nearby broken window. Furniture, covered in dusty gray cloth, sat upon the rotting carpets covering the floors.

She heaved out a sigh. *This was going to take a lot of work.*

Walking over to the staircase she put one foot on the first tread and leaned on it. Although it creaked it did not collapse. Natalie cautiously proceeded up the stairs, prepared to backtrack quickly if the steps gave way.

The stairs took her to three different floors which used to be guest rooms. *There're more rooms here than in the dormitory wing of the Abbey.*

She returned to the front door and stepped out on the veranda. "Staff please take the first floor of rooms, students, help yourself to rooms on the second and third floor. We're going to need to do repairs and clean-up. Despite the decay on the surface, the bones of the hotel seem quite strong. I know we just did a lot of this same work back home. But until home is safe, we might as well make this place livable."

Natalie contained her sigh of relief to a long slow exhale as, at last, people followed her orders with no mutters or furtive looks.

Once the last person filed in, Jake began his own inspection of his new home. *Time to follow my own orders.* Natalie slung her satchel over one shoulder, took Jules's hand and they went up to the first floor of the hotel. As they peered into various rooms, they saw various states of decay and disarray, the musty smell so overwhelming at times, they covered their noses.

At last they found a large suite of rooms in relatively good shape. There was a healthy coat of dust on everything, but dust cloths held the worst of it off the cloth furniture.

A sitting room with a cozy fireplace led into a large bedroom with a dark wooden four-poster bed that had an ornately carved headboard with matching wooden furniture. The ebony furniture contrasted beautifully with the light warmth of the wood floors.

With clasped hands they walked back to the sitting room and stepped through the two glass doors out onto the covered stone balcony. The sun peeked over the mountains and the lake shimmered under its glow. Birds conversed with one another in the trees and a gentle wind rustled the leaves.

Another wave of joy washed over Natalie. The hotel was a mess and her body rarely cooperated when she needed it to. Ystrelle held one friend captive, and another friend stayed behind at the Abbey to try and foil her attack. Yet a third friend's mental health was questionable.

She turned to Jules, only to see his face mirroring the cascade of happiness coursing through her.

Low, delicate chimes drifted across the lake and serenaded them on the balcony. Natalie's jaw dropped as she turned to the lake and back to Jules again.

He beamed down at her "Charlotte told me there's a small island in the middle of the lake with a bell tower. The bells ring every hour on the hour."

"It's beautiful," she whispered. Perhaps this place was old, forgotten and neglected but there was an undeniable magic about it. A magic not borne of mages and megaliths but of age-old construction and places that had once been magnificent and would be again.

Jules put his arms around her, and she turned in them, her lips finding his. She'd meant it to be a grateful, contented kiss, but Jules had other ideas. He tightened his arms, deepening the kiss, tongue flicking against her lower lip and his hand skimming along her spine.

A moan escaped her lips, and he captured it with his own. Bit by bit, Jules pushed her against the wall next to their balcony doors. He braced his palm against the wall to the left of her head and encircled her with his other arm, holding her spellbound.

Natalie wound her fingers through his hair capturing him for herself. She teased his lower lip with her teeth and then traced his jawline with kisses, her lips reveling in the sensation of his beard against her skin. Her hands slipped to the front buttons of his shirt when her mouth returned to his.

He groaned, pulling back and breaking off the kiss. Breathing heavily, he dipped his forehead to hers, lips swollen with their kisses. "Natalie, my love, I know the world is turning upside down. And you're still recovering." He ran the pad of his thumb across her cheek. "It's just that we've never … I have no idea what shape that bed is in there but … I want to …"

Natalie nodded, heart soaring. "I want you, too. Now," she demanded in between desperate kisses.

Drunk on their own ardor, they stumbled through the doors and into bed.

CHAPTER 17

Chimes echoed across the lake. Natalie's limbs tangled with Jules's, a smile playing on her lips when his arms tightened around her, fingertips trailing down her spine, leaving goose flesh in their wake.

His voice rumbled under her ear. "Good evening."

Natalie ran a toe up his calf. "Mm, yes indeed."

Jules kissed the top of her head, his lips lazily tracing a path down her temple and jaw to her lips. Natalie sighed, running her fingers through his hair.

A knock sounded at the door. "Headmistress Desmond," the knock came again louder this time. "Headmistress Desmond, are you in there?

"Hell in a kettle," Natalie swore, throwing the covers off.

"Come back to me soon, Headmistress," Jules smirked, folding his arms behind his head.

"Don't you go anywhere," she hissed over her shoulder

Natalie walked to the door and braced one hand against it in case the person had designs on coming in.

"What is it?"

"Thank Goddess. Headmistress Desmond, you're needed immediately. The runner from the Abbey is here, ma'am. Ystrelle has arrived. They're under attack."

Natalie swore again. "I'll be right down."

Jules swung out of bed, swearing himself. "So soon. I'd hoped for more time."

Natalie snatched her clothes from the haphazard pile on the floor, throwing the occasional piece of Jules's clothes at him. "Yeah, well if wishes were horses, we'd all be riding unicorns."

Natalie shoved her shirt into her waistband, deftly tied her leather bodice on, slid her feet into her boots and peered at herself in an old, chipped mirror covered with dark gray spots. Her clothing and hair were a mess and her face was red from making love.

Nothing for it. She sighed, swirling her cloak about her shoulders and striding for the door. "Meet me downstairs." Hand on the doorknob, she swore yet again.

"What is it?"

"Moonbark extract. I think I have some in my bag." Jogging over to her satchel and rummaging through it hastily, she found the dark bottle she needed and downed its contents in one gulp. "No need to bring a baby into this mess," she muttered, and dashed out the door.

"Where's the runner?" She demanded, entering the foyer.

"Here, Headmistress."

Sitting on what used to be the innkeeper's desk, a boy with a mop of messy ink-black hair sat drinking water from the canteen. The dust covering him from head to toe was a testament to how hard he'd ridden to reach them. To reach her.

"What's the news from the Abbey?"

The boy wiped his mouth with a dirty sleeve. "It took me an hour to ride here galloping as fast as was safe for my horse, Headmistress. I was scouting the woods as Mr. Onlo and Ms. Anli taught us to do. I saw the army coming up the road and recognized Ystrelle at its head from Ms. Anli's description. I ran through the woods as soft as I could, warned Ms. Anli, mounted and rode here."

"Good job. I'm glad you have something to drink. We'll get you something to eat as well,"

"There're already meals cooking outside on campfires, Headmistress. And where have you been these past few hours while the rest of us have been working?"

Putting her hands on her hips and facing Healer Edmundson, she ordered her face not to blush. After everything she and Jules had been through, no one had permission to give her trouble for a few stolen hours in his arms.

"Edmundson. Find the likeliest room for a hospital wing. Everyone else, we need to clean and supply the space that Healer Edmundson finds. We need to prepare for burn victims, folks. Let's go."

Natalie mentally kicked herself. *Orders I should've given when we first arrived. People* needed *me.*

But I needed him.

People scrambled from the room and she turned her back on Edmundson's glare.

Jules appeared next to her as she stepped outside and they went to each campfire taking an inventory of the food. Much to her pleasure, everyone had been very industrious and gathered what edible things remained from the fall woods. A few students from Anli's advanced class had shot a few deer with their bows and arrows. These same people told her they'd set trap lines throughout the woods.

"Great job, keep it up. We're going to need that food until we can re-establish trade with local farms. And merchants in Saltwick, too, if they'll come this far."

Natalie's heart gave an odd leap to see people pleased with her praise. She headed inside. "Let's go check on the progress of the hosp—"

"What's that?"

"Is it dawn?"

"No, it's too early; we'd have heard the chimes."

"Oh my Goddess, it must be the Abbey."

Natalie turned at the panicked voices, heart making an unnatural leap in her throat. There, on the eastern horizon, bloomed an ominous orange glow. Natalie recalled the last chimes she'd heard from the bell tower; it was just past midnight. The only thing in that direction that could make that much light was the Abbey.

It was on fire.

CHAPTER 18

Jules put his arms around Natalie as they watched the smoldering horizon, helpless to do anything to save their home. Anli and the people that had stayed behind to defend it were in the hands of fate. Em must be … where was Em? Natalie couldn't recall seeing her since arriving.

Jules bowed his head. "Five help us."

Tears flowed freely down Natalie's face and she let them. She'd spent close to half her life in that building. Met her best friend there. Met Jules and admired him from afar only to fall in love with him years later. The greenhouse where she spent her happiest hours—gone. Gayla's office, the library, all of it. Up in smoke.

A glint of silver caught her eye. Off to the side, next to one of the campfires, Queen Charlotte had gone to pieces.

The urge to curl up and sob pulled at Natalie like a strong undertow. But she was Headmistress; there was work to do.

She sucked in a shaky breath. "I know everyone is heartbroken," her voice wavered, but it carried across the clearing. "But Goddess willing, our e-ef-friends escaped. If they are injured, we need to be ready. This is our home now. There's no going back."

The bells tolled five in the morning as Natalie moved one more makeshift cot into place. She had to hand it to Healer Edmundson; he'd selected the hotel's cavernous old dining room as the new hospital. They'd converted each dining table into a patient bed using fresh, crisp white linens from the Abbey.

A brigade of staff offloaded supplies from the wagons, organizing them all in an old office just off the dining room. The hospital being in the dining room did create a problem for Cook, who was trying to make the old hotel kitchen work again. *I'll have to figure out where we'll take our meals later. Right now, I'm simply glad there's a working well outside the kitchen.*

The lack of sleep hounded her every move. She tried not to speak since she struggled more with words when exhausted. Wet sand seemed to fill every limb and it took all she had not to sink to the floor and fall asleep.

McKenna, fully recovered from her bout with kestrel fever, appeared in the hospital door. "Headmistress, they're here. The people from the Abbey."

Natalie abandoned her cot and strode for the door. "Thank you, McKenna."

Jogging down the steps, blinking as her eyes adjusted to the darkness, she followed torches to the road. Soot covered people limped toward her, some leading the more severely injured on horses.

"All right people, you know what to do. Get everyone into the hospital."

"Nat, help!"

Natalie turned and spotted Em leading a horse with a sack on its back.

"There you are. Did you—"

"It's Anli, please I need you."

Natalie's eyes widened; it wasn't a sack on the horse, it

was Anli.

Her friend hung limply astride the horse with her arms tied around its neck and each foot tied to the saddle to keep her on. Natalie seized a knot and began untying.

Em gingerly lifted one of Anli's arms. "I'll support her under this shoulder; that one's dislocated."

"All right, I'll help you and then support her torso."

"Be careful, I'm pretty sure she has broken ribs."

"Okay, I'll carry her legs."

"Watch out for the burns."

Goddess, what had happened back there? Em and Natalie pulled Anli, who slid off the horse. The horse spooked away and most of Anli's weight landed on Em, who collapsed under the weight of her lover.

Anli screamed.

"I need a stretcher, now," Natalie yelled. *Do we even have stretchers?*

Natalie clapped her hands on uninjured bits of her friend and Named her. *Holy Goddess, this is bad.*

Someone must've brought or made stretchers because a moment later, one appeared next to them. Removing her hands, she and Em transferred Anli onto the stretcher, and helped transport Anli in.

"Put her close to the supply room. Over here, over here," Natalie led her compatriots to a good location. With Anli now on one of the makeshift beds, Natalie completed her Naming.

Opening her eyes, she gazed at Em's somber face. "Multiple severe burns, a broken ankle, several broken ribs, and a dislocated shoulder.

Em nodded, lips trembling and tears spilling over. "She sacrificed herself to save my life. I would be dead if she didn't shove me out of the way when she did."

Natalie hugged her best friend. "Go get some food and water. I'll take care of her."

Taking advantage of Anli's unconscious state, Natalie bent Anli's arm at the correct angle, and pulled until the joint went back to its proper place.

Over the next two hours, Natalie treated all of Anli's wounds, setting and wrapping her ankle, covering her burns with mashed solenloe leaf and bandaging them. With Jules's help, she wrapped Anli's broken ribs and immobilized her shoulder joint. They managed to trickle some dullanbark tea down her throat, which Natalie Activated along with the solenloe. She gazed at Anli, tears stinging the corners of her eyes. *Thank you. Thank you for nearly giving your life to defend my home.*

Bracing her hands on the table, Natalie raised her head and peered around the room, now illuminated by the sun rising over the lake. Roughly thirty patients covered the erstwhile dining tables. "I'm going to—"

"You're going to sit down before you fall down," Jules said in a low tone. "I know how concerned you are about appearances. So sit here next to Anli—" he pulled up one of the dining chairs, "—and keep an eye on her. What needs to be done?"

Natalie lowered herself into the chair, tears of gratitude and frustration pricking her eyes. "The other patients. How are they doing? Who is the worst and what supplies do we need?"

Jules nodded and squeezed her shoulder. "I'll find out."

Helplessness washed over Natalie as she sat next to Anli, putting her elbow on the table and resting her head in her hand. Her body had progressed from wet sand to jelly. If she stood, she'd look like a newborn foal trying to take its first steps. *I'm sure Head Councilwoman Ramesh is* so *glad she made me Headmistress. I can't keep up with the work. Oh and let's not forget that one month in and the Abbey is gone.*

Em emerged from the shadows. "Will she be all right?"

Natalie let her hand slide from her face over her hair. "We have to watch out for fever, but yes I think so."

Em gingerly twined her fingers with Anli's. "We were talking about getting married."

"So soon?" Natalie couldn't help herself. They'd just met

this past spring.

"Yes, well. When you know, you know," Em whispered to her and Anli's clasped hands.

"Then you will get married," Natalie replied with a stubborn ring in her voice.

"It was horrible there. I thought I'd seen horrible things this past summer, but this was …" Em shook her head. "She was livid when she found I'd stayed behind. We fought and then Ystrelle … none of us would've survived without Anli. She put traps throughout the forest and even the Abbey itself so that the thirty of us could hold out as long as we did. She organized everyone, made sure they knew what to do and what the fall back positions were. The Abbey would've gone up in flames immediately if it wasn't for her.

"For a while, we thought we might have a chance, but in the end, they just kept coming. We were at the last fallback position, surrounded by fire when she dove in front of a fire mage to save me. We all just grabbed her and ran."

Natalie creaked to a standing position and hugged Em from behind. "Everyone there did amazing."

"I'm a Healer, Natalie. I've never wanted kill anyone. I want to kill Ystrelle," Em covered her quiet sobs with her free hand.

Natalie rocked her friend back and forth. "Shh, I know, I know." She murmured comforts to Em all the while keeping an eye on Anli. Her breathing was shallow but steady. Natalie helped Em to the chair she'd recently vacated. "If I ask you to o-wo-watch over her, will that make it better or worse?"

Em gave her a watery smile. "Better."

"Okay. But you must leave her side at some point to sleep and eat, understood? You cannot take care of her if you're not taking care of yourself."

Em nodded and Natalie scanned the rest of the room. She spied Jules and made a beeline for him seeking a status on the casualties.

As she arrived, Jules and the Healer he was working with pulled the sheet up over the person on the table. All the way over their head. Her stomach sank to her toes. *No. This person bought time for her and everyone else to get to Lake Clanairys. With their life.*

She met Jules's gaze, his emerald eyes shining with unshed tears. They said nothing; they simply clasped hands and held on tight.

Walking out to the porch, admiring the campfires in the morning light, Natalie drew a shuddering breath. "What of the other casualties? Did anyone else die?"

"Two people died in the assault on the Abbey itself," Jules began.

Part of Natalie felt like two was a low number. Thirty people versus Ystrelle and her army of mages and Queensguard and they'd only lost two?

On the other hand, it felt like two too many. She'd asked people to stay behind, they volunteered willingly—*and died. To protect us.*

"We just lost another as you saw. Another three patients are in critical condition."

"Who?" Natalie demanded. She needed to know their names. No one would forget the sacrifice of these thirty people.

Jules told her and she nodded. Natalie stifled a yawn. "Let's get back in there, then."

Warm fingers caught her elbow. "Natalie, you need sleep. Let's trust our staff; the people Gayla trained."

"I can't, I must—"

"Natalie, how can you be in charge of all these people if you are dead on your feet?"

Sauce for the goose. Did he know I just said the same thing to Em?

She acquiesced. After stopping to let the hospital Healers know they needed a break, hand in hand, they ascended the stairs to their new retreat and were asleep before their heads hit the pillow.

CHAPTER 19

"There's people in black coming up the road, ma'am," a gangly teenage boy rushed back out of the hospital as soon as he came in. Natalie's heart pounded. *Ystrelle. No, wait. People in* black.

She looked up from the bandages she was changing. "Obfuselt? Healer Bishop, please take over for me."

Handing her supplies to Healer Bishop, Natalie dashed outside and ran toward the road. Laughter and tears erupted when she spotted several familiar faces.

"Mysha! Mysha Harris!" She grabbed the Obfuseltan woman, whom she'd helped nurse through a difficult pregnancy last summer, and drew her into a hug. "I'm so sorry, I'm probably covered in blood. Shepherd, how are you? And is this little Emma?" Natalie grinned at the plump, rosy-cheeked baby eying her with suspicion from the sling on Shepherd's back.

"That's her. Quiet for now, but give it time and you'll hear her dulcet tones for sure."

"We received word from the Council of Isles a week or

so ago. We heard you could use help," Shepherd said.

"I will send all the help I can," the Head Councilwoman had said when Charlotte arrived at the Abbey. It was all Natalie could do not to break down in front of everyone. "Yes! Your help is *most* welcome."

Mysha eyed the old hotel skeptically. "That's some building you've got there."

Natalie dabbed her eyes on a clean bit of sleeve. "It is indeed. Cobwebs everywhere, moldy old furniture and peeling paint. But we don't fall through the stairs when we walk on them so there's that."

Mysha cocked an eyebrow. "Perhaps there's some hope after all. Come on everyone, let's get set up."

"I'll show you where the food and rooms are," Natalie gestured for the black clad entourage to proceed.

A tallish boy with hair very similar to her own made her do a double take. He was staring pointedly at the ground, so she had to bend to the side to confirm what she saw.

"Aaron? Aaron Desmond, what are you doing here?"

Her brother's head snapped up, his face turning an astonishing shade of magenta. "I … I'm here to help rebuild."

Natalie crossed her arms and put her face right in his. He'd grown an incredible amount since the summer and she could now look him directly in the eye. "And where is Mother?"

"Home?" he asked, voice cracking.

"You don't know for sure? What did you *do*, Aaron Desmond?"

He held up his hands, backing away. "I always said I wanted to see if I'd Attune to Obfuselt."

She took in his black clad appearance. Everyone was staring at them now. Natalie didn't care. Her little brother was in the muck pile so deep he'd be digging himself out until next fall.

"So you left Mother *alone*? You tell me what happened to her, Aaron Desmond or so help me I will have Jules blast you back home myself."

"I … I ran away. Mother's not alone, she has Ms. Siobhan from Solerin helping her run the farm. I went to Obfuselt, planning to return if the Isle didn't take me. But it did and so I wrote her a letter."

Natalie's voice raised another octave. "You. Wrote. Her. A *letter?*"

A hand came down on her shoulder and Natalie turned, fists clenched, ready to knock the person into next week.

"Try not to be so hard on the lad, Natalie," Shepherd said. "He felt terribly guilty about it and he wrote may letters home. Your Mother was angry that he ran away, but, judging from her letters, she supports his new path."

"I can show you her letters, Nat."

Natalie pinched the bridge of her nose and counted to ten. "Okay. Go get food and lodging with the rest."

He walked away, and it dawned on Natalie how grown up he looked. When had that happened? *When I was fighting epidemics and power hungry sociopaths, apparently.*

"You always did have a way with children." A tall woman with long dark hair, burnished tan-colored skin and striking topaz eyes followed the rest, though she was not dressed in black.

"Siaraa!" Natalie hugged the woman who'd helped her build so many rat traps in Roseharbor last spring. Siaraa backed out of the embrace.

"Hey, no affection now. People will think I've gone soft."

"Not a chance. It's so good to see you."

Siaraa eyed the hotel askance. "Is this the new Abbey?"

Natalie peered over her shoulder. "It's all we've got."

"Well, then. Let's make it a proper one, shall we?"

CHAPTER 20

Standing by the lake, Natalie marveled at the difference a week made. The hotel, instead of smelling like rot and mold, now smelled like saw dust and fresh wood and paint.

Of the twenty-seven people who survived Ystrelle's decimation of the Abbey, most were up and walking within a day of arrival. Some, like Anli, were still in bed, sedated to avoid aggravating their injuries.

Anli had a nasty bout with a fever that kept Jules, Em and Natalie by her side for thirty-six hours straight. At last, they were able to lower her body temperature, at one point even treating her outside in the chilly weather.

The fever had slowed her Healing process, but Natalie's gut feeling was that Anli was almost out of the woods.

Deciding one more check on her friend wouldn't hurt, she called Jake, who stood with his paws in the water, wistfully gazing out at the lake in hopes of a swim.

Ascending the stairs of the hotel's front veranda, Natalie trailed her hand along the freshly reconstructed railing installed by her amazing friends from Obfuselt.

"A moment of your time, Headmistress?"

"Healer Bowers. Sure, what do you need?"

Healer Bowers gave her a narrow look. "Best if we talk in the new animal sanctuary."

Oh. She might have a treatment for my head. "Why—of-of, course, let me come with you."

Natalie followed Healer Bowers to what used to be a screened-in section of the sprawling veranda. The construction workers converted it into a bifurcated space, leaving one part exposed to the outdoors for those animals ready for a more natural environment. Solid walls enclosed the rest with an iron stove keeping the space cozy warm.

Healer Bowers handed her a bunch of dried leaves. "Here. But use only a little every evening for your head."

"Fidelia weed? But we use this for anesthesia during surgery."

"Which is why I said only use a little," Healer Bowers replied as if Natalie was a child and hadn't listened to the directions.

"But you're talking about casual use of fidelia," Natalie hissed. "We've seen people get addicted that way."

"You've seen people addicted to ale and wine. Does that stop you from drinking a pint when you go to the pub?"

Natalie blinked. She hadn't thought of it that way.

"Of course not," Healer Bowers said. "Look, I managed to do some research before we left and I've dug through my own notes on how I treated animals with head injuries. This is often my only option to keep them comfortable. Don't use enough to make you fall asleep, only enough to make you pleasant and relaxed. See if it helps. Hell, let me know if it helps. You'll be my first patient who can actually tell me how it's going."

Natalie huffed out a breath, frowning at the leaves in her palm. "All right. I've got nothing to lose."

Entering the hospital for her promised check on Anli, Natalie smiled at the sight of proper beds, topped with mattresses stuffed full of dried fall grasses and encased in crisp white linen. With all the updates to the old hotel, Natalie could really see a future here. Classes, a library, gardens, a greenhouse; a center for Healing as the Abbey had once been.

Only the Council of Isles knew where they were, but they hardly dared broadcast their location yet. *I'm scared for the rest of Ismereld. What if they need our hospital? I'll just have to hope the local Healers can help. Ystrelle will find out soon enough where we are, though how we'll survive another attack, I have no idea.*

Looking up from Anli, who rested comfortably, she caught Jules staring at her from across the room. He leaned casually against a window, one elbow resting on the sill, one leg crossed over the other. Natalie felt her cheeks reddening. Desire burned in his emerald eyes; Her heart pounded in her ears and she struggled to catch her breath.

She jumped as a passing Healer bumped into her.

"Sorry, *Headmistress*," Healer Brendon Edmundson's sarcastic voice broke the spell.

Her eyes darted back to the window. Jules caught her eye, winked and left the room. She returned her attention to Anli, checking bandages she knew were perfectly fine and tucking in the already snug sheets.

When she judged enough time had passed, she gave a furtive glance around the room, muttered a prayer that no one was paying attention, made for the exit and ran up the stairs.

Gasping for breath, she opened the door to their newly painted suite. Jules grabbed her by the waist and swung her around, kissing her so deeply she felt it all the way down in her toes. When he set her down, she pressed him against the door, closing it. Natalie fumbled for the lock and turned it before seizing the front of his shirt and pulling him to her.

CHAPTER 21

Natalie flung an arm over her face when the pounding didn't go away. *I know there's been a lot of construction, but hearing hammering in my sleep is too much.*

"Headmistress?" a muffled voice came from the door.

"Hell in a bloody kettle, I can't get a break," she muttered. Raising her head from Jules's shoulder, she called out: "Yes?"

"Someone has arrived to see you."

Natalie flopped back on her own pillow, closing her eyes and breathing through her nose. "Tell them I'll be down in five minutes." She turned to Jules and rested her forehead against his. "I'm sorry."

His hand pushed against her shoulder and she leaned back, meeting his deep, emerald eyes. "Natalie, we've been through so much the past year. I'm grateful for every moment we have together. Go. Do your job."

She traced her fingers along his jawline. "I'm so glad you're here. I couldn't have done all this without you. You make me so happy."

Why don't we get married like Em and Anli?

Her heart skittered. Where did that thought come from? She and Jules had been to hell and back together but ... marriage?

"What is it? You were smiling and now something's troubling you."

"Nothing, I just need to go see who is here."

After dressing and doing her hair in its customary braid, Natalie made sure she looked presentable in their brand new mirror before heading downstairs with Jake, butterflies doing somersaults in her stomach.

What made her think of marriage? Why did it make her nervous? She loved Jules, didn't she?

"Headmistress."

Natalie's feet slowed to a stop on the stairs at the sight of the dark haired, colorfully garbed woman at the bottom of the stairs. "Head Councilwoman," she choked. *Oh Goddess. Last time I saw Geeta Ramesh, we'd just learned of the impending attack on the Abbey—and now it's gone.*

Natalie stood in front of the Head Councilwoman, heart in her throat and thrumming at an alarming speed. She knew she should say something polite and welcoming, but the words refused to come out.

"Please show me your new facilities."

"Of-of course. Please, follow me." Natalie took the Head Councilwoman on a tour of the former hotel, Jake's nose twitching as he surveyed all from a distance. Pride welled up in her as she pointed out changes and improvements. The Councilwoman's face remained inscrutable.

"We've made the best of our situation," Natalie hedged.

The Head Councilwoman nodded. "I'm pleased, However, the situation is worse than you know."

Natalie rubbed her eyes. "My, I never would have guessed. What can you tell me?"

Natalie assembled Jules, Em, Queen Charlotte and Mysha—her most trusted friends and confidantes—to hear what the Head Councilwoman had to say. They gathered in the empty space that would become the Headmistress's—her—office.

"Ystrelle is preparing to take over all of the Isles,"

Natalie glanced at Charlotte. Did she know this? The queen crossed her arms and stared at the floor.

"She's training her mages. Apparently she's listened to Jyrenn's lessons so many times, she's memorized them."

Jules swore.

"The other council members and I agree she must be stopped."

Natalie barely contained an undignified snort. *Was there a two-hour meeting to decide the psychopathic ex-councilwoman must be stopped?*

"We want Juliers Rayvenwood and Queen Charlotte Fairisles to pursue and contain her. Kill her if necessary."

"Why them? They've done enough."

"It can't be done." Charlotte stated.

"You must, my queen."

"Why them?" Natalie repeated.

"The queen and Healer Mage Rayvenwood are more experienced than any mage she has. We must restore the queen to power. You are the only mages capable of facing her army."

"Two mages against her army?"

"If I may," Mysha spoke for the first time, "two mages going after Ystrelle and her army might be suicidal. But if she they came here? There might be a chance." She rested her chin on her palm.

Natalie's jaw dropped. "Mysha, you're helping rebuild this place, now you want a crazy woman to attack it?"

"What's your plan?" Jules asked.

"Well, the old Abbey was, unfortunately, indefensible. I've heard stories of Anli's efforts and I think she did everything possible—even some things I wouldn't have thought of. But in the end, it was a building in the wide open surrounded by a forest where people and artillery could hide.

"This hotel, however, is surrounded by mountains on three sides and water on the other. The only way in is on the road. My Isles' team can build defenses. The road needs a gate. Where possible, we need walls with guards."

Natalie blinked in disbelief. "You're talking about a fort."

"Yes."

"But this isn't a military operation; it's a place of Healing and learning."

Em put her head in her palms. "So was the Abbey. And now it's a heap of charred rubble."

No retort came to mind so Natalie sat arms crossed and stared at the wood dust on the floor.

Jules sighed. "I don't like it. But we should do it."

Em turned to Mysha. "What do you have in mind for defenses?"

Natalie gaped at the pair as Mysha explained how her team could gather rocks from the surrounding mountains and build a wall across where the road came in.

"I don't know how much time we have, but we can build a gate. It will be simple at first but we can replace it with increasingly impenetrable ones if Ystrelle gives us the time."

"A stone wall? Ystrelle destroyed the Abbey, and that was *made* of stone. We need something better," Em argued.

"We don't have time for something better. If we were on Obfuselt and could use our magic and had a larger team, we could come up with something that might counter artillery—"

"And mages," Charlotte added.

Mysha nodded. "But here? A stone wall is your best option."

"But this is Ismereld, not Ebenos Point Keep or even Roseharbor for that matter. Since the time of Bridhe, this has been a pe-pl-place of peace. I don't want to be Headmistress of a fort."

"Times have changed whether you wanted them to or

not, Headmistress Desmond," the Head Councilwoman pointed out. "You've been asking people to adapt to change since you took over. It would set a poor example if you yourself could not do the same."

Natalie blinked, chagrined. "Charlotte, you said pursuing Ystrelle and her army wouldn't work. Why?"

Charlotte chewed on her pinky nail. Her left heel bounced as if she was keeping time to rapid music only she could hear. "You need numbers and power. You know she has mages, an army and explosives. I think they'll be here soon. So we need more. Archers who can fire on the mages. I don't think they'll be experienced enough to magically attack the arrows before they hit their targets. Not if Ystrelle is training them and they've never had to use their powers in battle."

Jules sat with his arms crossed, head resting on his hand with one finger tapping the side of his cheek. "The mages I'm training show a lot of promise. I don't know if they're battle ready, but I can start doing drills with them. Perhaps the mages can take out the munitions before Ystrelle's army has a chance to use them."

"I could send to Obfuselt for reinforcements. They'd be here within two or three days of getting the message," Mysha added.

Natalie put her head in her hands. "How can I ask my students to become killers when they came here to learn Healing? It was hard enough for me to swallow learning self-defense."

"We'll only attack if they attack first, sweeting," Em said, putting a hand on her arm. "I know it's hard. But the sight of our Abbey in flames is one I will never forget. I'll do anything to save what whatever's left."

Natalie grasped Em's hand and squeezed it. "Okay. Okay. What do we do first?"

"C'mon Nat, help us out."

"No, thank you, Aaron, I'm just fine right here," Natalie drew her winter cloak around her shoulders and pulled her fur-lined hood up over her head, shivering in the late fall air. She, Em, Anli and Charlotte watched the black-clad Obfuseltans, most of whom were sweating and wearing short sleeves, as they constructed the wall across the road.

With the reinforcements that Mysha ordered, the wall was going up in no time. From a sketch she had examined, Natalie knew the wall would eventually have a fortified gate and two watch towers with openings for archers or mages to fire through. *If necessary.*

"She'll be coming soon," Charlotte said. Her flat, detached voice had returned soon after the Head Councilwoman left. The very sound of it always made the bottom drop out of Natalie's heart and sent a ripple of unease down her spine. Would her queen ever recover from her imprisonment?

But the queen was correct. Natalie had resumed trade with local farmers and vendors in Saltwick for food and other necessities. It was that or deplete the local wild and plant life, a notion she found unacceptable. *Besides, anyone with a hint of tracking talent could find us.* Everyone *knows where we are. It's only a matter of time.*

Em put her arm around Charlotte. "You know what I think? I think we need a name for this place. It just doesn't seem right to call it Bridhe of the Isles Abbey."

"How about Bridhe of the Isles Old Hotel?" Natalie suggested, putting her arm around both her friends.

Charlotte gave a most un-queen-like snort.

"Have you been hit on the head during construction?" Anli asked.

Quite the opposite. She'd started using a bit of fidelia weed in the evenings, as Healer Bowers had suggested. She was down to only one or two migraines a week. Even her fatigue eased up just a bit.

"Bridhe's Healing School and Hospital?" Em suggested.

"Too plain," Natalie observed. "Come on, let's go see how the mages are doing."

Em helped Anli, who'd finally been allowed out of bed after several days of loud complaining, over to the field next to the lake.

Jules worked on target practice with the mages starting with large dummies and working down to smaller and smaller targets. The mages worked in pairs, one person throwing a stone in the air and their partner trying to hit it. Natalie feared for the nearby trees as bolts of lightning, jets of fire and shards of ice and rock flew back and forth. *So much for not teaching offensive magery.*

Glancing at Jules though, she couldn't help but grin like the lovesick schoolgirl she'd once been. He strode between the students, the fall sun shining on his dark hair, adjusting technique here and giving praise there. Jules's work paid off in spades; his students handled their difficult and dangerous tasks with grace.

Natalie forced her feet to stay put rather than walking into the class, taking his hand and dragging him to their room. Instead she cocked an eyebrow at her friends. "I guess we're no longer just a school of Healing."

"You're not kidding," Em said, eyes wide as saucers.

"The Bridhe Center for Healing and Magical Arts," Natalie said, turning back to look at the old hotel. It positively gleamed compared to when she'd first set eyes on it. They had even built a few classrooms inside so the youngest children could return to class while the older ones helped with restoration or trained.

Em nodded. "I love it."

"It's perfect," The queen agreed.

Anli shrugged. "I guess you have good ideas once in a while, Headmistress."

CHAPTER 22

"A rmy on the road!" someone inside the Center shouted, relaying the message sent by the watchtower at the gate.

Natalie looked up from her patient in the hospital. *It's time. Ystrelle's here.*

Donning a short, emerald winter cape and grasping a short staff she'd taken to carrying, she walked to the gate, heart thrumming in the vicinity of her throat. *I'm glad my friends talked me into building the fortifications. Otherwise, that army would already be upon a lot of vulnerable people.*

Jules appeared beside her and grasped her hand. She halted, cupped his face with her hands and drew his head down to hers, kissing him thoroughly and not caring one whit if anyone saw. When they pulled apart, he tucked a stray lock of hair behind her ear. "I love you."

"I love you, too."

"Do you remember the plan?"

"Yes," she said on a sharp exhale. Remembering was one thing. Making it happen was another. *Would it work? The Five only knew.*

As Natalie approached the gate, she comforted herself with the thought of the students and staff not participating in the fight slipping out the back door of the Center and up into the mountains. Even now, archers and mages crept through the forest into camouflaged locations.

She and Jules climbed the freshly hewn watch tower stairs knowing they'd find people ready to defend the Center with their weapons, skills—or lives.

Natalie reached the top of the tower and put her hand on Mysha's shoulder. Mysha, the appointed leader of the Center's defenses, turned to Natalie, her mouth drawn in a thin line. Pursing her lips, Natalie squinted through one of the narrow slits built for the archers. Ystrelle stood at the head of the army, mounted on her majestic gray stallion. Behind her was the Royal Army and on either side of her...

A string of curses that would impress any Obfuselt sailor came out of Jules's mouth, one floor above her with the other mages

Mounted on matching bay steeds on either side of Ystrelle, Jules's parents stared defiantly at the gate. *Hell in a kettle.*

"Welcome to the Bridhe Center for Healing and Magical Arts, how can we help you?" Natalie shouted toward the party.

Ystrelle nudged her stallion forward. "We've come for Mage Juliers Rayvenwood and Natalie Desmond."

Natalie snorted. "I'm sorry, we can't help you."

"Come now, Natalie. We both know I can take down this meager wall and destroy you all."

It had taken Natalie a long time to get used to people calling her "Headmistress". Now her blood simmered at Ystrelle's refusal to acknowledge her title.

"Ystrelle, go home to Jyrenn and let the mages and their families go. You've done enough."

Ystrelle's face softened at the mention of Jyrenn, but the hard lines returned in an instant.

"I'm here *for* Jyrenn," Ystrelle declared and whirled her horse, issuing orders Natalie couldn't hear. The horses retreated to the back of the army, revealing four ominous looking carts lumbered to the front of the crowd.

Those carts destroyed my Abbey.

"Jules?" Mysha called out.

"Mages ready," Jules replied.

Natalie's heart hammered in her ears as she watched the front line mages cock their arms, hands bristling with magic. A tall lanky man with pale skin and matted hair approached one of the carts with a torch and a mad expression on his face.

Goddess damn it all, no one was going to die here if she could help it. She nodded to Mysha.

"Take the carts out," Mysha ordered.

A volley of ice and stone flew overhead. "Nice," Natalie hissed as the carts crumpled beneath the attack.

And then they exploded.

Natalie found herself pinned to the floor by the archers on either side of her. A piercing whine filled her ears. For one terrible moment, she was back in the sea after their ship had been blown out of the water by the New Mage's Guild, trying to stay afloat. And breathe. Just breathe.

I can't breathe, I have two people on top of me.

"Are you all right, Headmistress?" The voice came from near her left ear.

Thank the Five I can still hear. The archers protected me from the explosions with their own bodies. Oh Goddess are they hurt? She waved her hand, and they scrambled off her, helping her up.

"Are you okay?" she looked at each one but, aside from a healthy dusting of dirt, they were unharmed.

She looked out at the road; a large crater lay where the carts had once been. Flames licked up several nearby trees, devouring the dead, dry leaves.

Oh Goddess, Mysha and I stationed mages and archers in those trees. Several burned bodies lay scattered about the blast area; some still and some writhing and crying in pain.

Natalie clenched her fists. "We didn't hit them with fire or electricity, why did the carts explode?" Natalie asked Mysha over the twang of bowstrings and the shouts of the mages above as they engaged the army.

"Ystrelle's fire mages lit them up."

What sort of hold does this woman have on these people that they're willing to commit suicide for her?

Natalie checked for her short staff in its holster on her back. There was nothing she could do up here but wait. When she spotted arrows and magical attacks falling on the army from the nearby trees, her chest heaved with relief; the blast hadn't killed everyone along the road, thank the Five.

She ducked just in time as a fireball from one of Ystrelle's mages hit the outside tower wall. The timber building caught fire instantly.

"Fire!" Natalie shouted along with several others. "Out, out, get out!" She moved people toward the stairway with her hands. The mages came down from above; Jules was the last one down.

"Upstairs is clear," he coughed.

They clasped hands and followed everyone down, moving toward the other tower just in time to see it take a bolt of electricity and a fire ball at the same time. The people in that tower spilled out to meet them. They regrouped several yards back from the gate away from the smoke. The Obfuseltan-steel reinforced gate shuddered as Ystrelle's forces attacked.

"They're going to get through."

"Your Majesty, you should be with the people leaving the fort," Mysha protested.

"I must stay," Charlotte replied in the dead voice Natalie hated.

Jules drew his sleeve across his creased forehead. "Are you saying you want to fight?"

"I must stay," she repeated.

"That's—"

"You can't—"

"We don't have time for this," Mysha interrupted. "Mages, what's your status energy-wise?" She listened while quickly tending a shallow gash on Shepherd's cheek.

Jules glanced around his team. "Pretty depleted I'd say. We countered our fair share of mage attacks. Surely their mages are just as tired."

Natalie and Jules held each other's gaze for the briefest moment. *Should we combine our energies as we did in the throne room at Roseharbor? To defeat Ystrelle, maybe we should...*

Jules shook his head ever so slightly. From the expression on his face, she could tell he wouldn't risk it for the world.

"We'll have to take this fight out of the gate and engage them in hand to hand combat. Do they have archers?"

"Not that I saw. I believe Ystrelle put all her faith in her mages and artillery."

"At least they destroyed their artillery," Mysha sighed. "All right, here's how we get out there without them picking us off one by one. We open the gate and let them in."

Natalie blinked. "What?"

"Just a bit, you see. The gate will act like a bottleneck and only a few will get through at a time. We'll pick them off as they come through."

There was a boulder that Mysha had placed nearby in case of this very eventuality; it would hold the gate open only partway forcing Ystrelle's army to come through nearly single file.

Several people rolled the large stone into place. Mysha gave the order for everyone to take up their positions.

Much to her chagrin, Natalie was at the back, guarded by two people. Sighing, she had to admit it was for the best. She'd been so busy being Headmistress and overseeing the transformation of the hotel that she'd rarely sparred or kept up with her training; she was a liability. Nevertheless, she dug her nails into her short staff, bouncing on her toes and warming up her muscles.

"Now!" Mysha shouted.

The mages and archers easily picked off the first several foes. As more streamed through, it got harder and harder; Mysha's forces resorted to hand to hand combat.

Uselessness such as she hadn't felt since her exile on Obfuselt threatened to overwhelm Natalie. All she was doing was hiding behind her guards while her people fought and died to protect the Center as the smoke from the burning towers plumed into the sky.

Jules was a whirling blur of blue electricity and daggers and even Queen Charlotte joined the fray, burning anyone who got in her path into a crisp.

One of Natalie's guards took her elbow. "Headmistress, let's get you back to the Healers."

Tempting as that was—she would certainly be more useful as a Healer right now—she couldn't leave the battle. She couldn't leave Jules's side and she wanted to keep an eye on Charlotte, whose dispassionate decimation of their foes chilled Natalie's soul.

She was the Headmistress, and she owed it to all of them to stay. Plus, she had a score to settle with Ystrelle.

Enough people came through the gate that even Natalie's guards engaged in battle. Natalie managed to get a few blows in with her staff, knowing she'd feel it later. If she was still alive.

With this last surge, people stopped coming through the gate. Blinking in disbelief, Natalie did a quick scan of their side of the battle. Mysha, Shepherd and Jules breathed heavily, but still lived.

Charlotte didn't even have a speck of blood on her; she looked as though she'd just gotten up from having tea. She strode over to Natalie, who surveyed the rest of the carnage while Mysha and several other people closed the gate.

Bodies littered the ground and a few more cracks formed in Natalie's heart as she surveyed the carnage. The tattered uniforms of The Royal Army fluttered in the biting wind alongside emerald and black cloaks, singed and bloody.

The Royal Army used to be the loyal servants of the king

and queen—until Ystrelle got ahold of them and conscripted them for her own purpose.

And Ystrelle's mages. *They were just people who happened to survive the sweating epidemic and develop magical powers. If only we'd gotten to them sooner.* Now the family member held hostage at Roseharbor will never see their loved one again.

And where was Ystrelle? What was she waiting for?

"Charlotte," she said as the queen arrived beside her. "Why did Ystrelle allow us to kill so much of her Army?"

"Natalie Desmond," Ystrelle's voice echoed along the road. "Come out now and bring Mage Rayvenwood with you."

"Go to hell!"

"Do as she says, Natalie."

"Charlotte," Jules choked.

The queen's palms faced Natalie, crackling with flame.

CHAPTER 23

"Move and I'll kill Natalie and take you to her myself, Jules," Charlotte said, her voice void of inflection or feeling.

"Charlotte, sweeting? Why are you doing this?"

Charlotte's hand swung around. "Natalie move, or I'll kill Mysha."

Natalie lifted her hands, palms facing her queen. "Okay, okay, don't kill anyone. I'll go."

"Nat, no!"

"You will go too, Jules," Charlotte ordered.

Mysha opened the gate and Natalie stepped over the body of one of the archers who'd protected her when the artillery carts exploded. She strode toward Ystrelle, chin up.

Inside, her soul ice covered her soul. When had Charlotte betrayed them? She'd been raving when she'd arrived at the Abbey; on the edge of madness. Had Ystrelle sent her to betray them? Or maybe she really had gone mad.

Mounted atop her stallion, with Jules's parents alongside, Ystrelle rode toward her. Natalie peeked between them. About fifteen of Ystrelle's army remained.

So few. We outnumber her, now. What does she think will happen here? If Charlotte kills me, the joint Ismereld-Obfuselt force will certainly decimate them.

"Surrender," Ystrelle demanded.

"I accept your surrender," Natalie smirked.

Blood suffused Ystrelle's face. "I will take Mage Rayvenwood with me despite your attitude, young lady."

"No you bloody won't."

"Language, Juliers," this from Jules's mother on her bay palfrey.

"Shut up. You disowned me anyway, what do you care?"

"Ystrelle has plans for you, son," Jules's father explained, as if this justified all that had taken place.

"Tough shit."

Ystrelle turned to Charlotte. "My queen, if you please."

Charlotte drew back her hands, palms facing Natalie and summoned her flames. "Go, Juliers. Go, or I'll kill her."

"Charlotte, this isn't you. Remember our lessons together with Jyrenn?" Jules pled. "He wouldn't want this."

"You *dare* mention his name. Charlotte, kill her," Ystrelle ordered.

The fire between her fingers intensified and Charlotte took a step back, ready to attack. Her face cracked and tears spilled over her eyes.

"I-I-can't, my lady."

Ystrelle signaled with one hand. Two men brought someone, bound and gagged, to the front of the ranks. Natalie's jaw dropped.

"Onlo," Charlotte sobbed.

Ystrelle dismounted and approached Onlo, drawing a large dagger with a jewel-encrusted handle. Stepping behind him, she grabbed his chin and pressed the blade against his exposed throat. A bead of red blood trickled down Onlo's dark skin.

Natalie saw with horror that his neck sported several long, thin horizontal scars. Obviously not the first time he'd had a dagger at his throat while in Ystrelle's custody. Given the love between Charlotte and Onlo, no wonder Charlotte did Ystrelle's bidding.

Ystrelle drew the blade ever so slightly across his throat. "Kill. Her."

Charlotte, sobbing openly now, turned back to Natalie, who gazed at her queen and former student in terror. A blue light erupted from behind Charlotte and she slumped to the ground. Natalie saw Jules fire another bolt at Ystrelle. Ystrelle ducked.

"Charge!"

Natalie didn't need Mysha to tell her twice. She grabbed her staff and ran with her people, directly at Ystrelle; she'd pay for what she'd done.

Ystrelle's remaining forces surrounded her and Natalie let her mind slip into months of Onlo's relentless training as she whirled, struck, parried and fought her way to her quarry.

All too soon, her initial battle frenzy ran out and her body reminded her she hadn't really trained in months. Fatigue slowed her movements and rooted her in place. *I'll never make it, Goddess damn it, I'm a danger to myself and others out here.* When defeat nearly pulled her to her knees, she saw an opening beyond which stood Ystrelle.

Willing her body to give one last effort, she charged through the sea of bodies and weapons and leaped on Ystrelle, sweeping her legs out from under her and pointing her staff at her throat.

"Stop!" Charlotte's voice commanded.

Out of habit, Natalie obeyed. She turned to her queen as Ystrelle yanked her staff away. Charlotte, only knocked unconscious by Jules's bolt, now held Jules himself with one orange-red tinged palm inches from his face.

"Or I'll kill him."

Natalie put her palms up, which someone seized and tied behind her back at the wrists.

"Tie Mage Rayvenwood's arms to his body. Then tie him

and Miss Desmond to horses. Gag them," Ystrelle ordered brushing dirt off her expensive robes.

Heart pounding somewhere in her throat, Natalie choked and willed herself not to vomit as a guard forced a great wad of cloth into her mouth. Her instincts screamed at her to struggle as someone forced her onto a horse. Some remaining part of her brain told her to submit; she didn't want Jules to die.

Mounted alongside Ystrelle and Jules's parents, Natalie shot a wide-eyed glance at Mysha, who stood in the road, arms crossed. Mysha's head inclined forward ever so slightly as their eyes met. *She's up to something. She'll come find us, I know it.*

Ystrelle gave the order to move out. "Kill the rest."

The gag didn't stop Natalie from screaming when they killed Mysha and Shepherd.

CHAPTER 24

Ystrelle hadn't deigned to tell her prisoners their destination so the familiar streets of Saltwick were a sight for sore eyes. They stopped for the night at an upscale inn. To the outside observer, Natalie figured their party looked very fascinating; The queen, two of Roseharbor's elite citizens with their son, a Healer and their guards.

What people couldn't see was her bound hands under the luxurious brown fur cloak Ystrelle gave her. "I can't have you dying from the cold," she'd smirked.

She wanted to shout at everyone in the inn about Ystrelle's treachery. But it would mean her instant death at the hands of the guards behind her. So she kept quiet, panic bubbling up as her guard led her up the stairs and to a separate room from Jules. She shot him a desperate glance as his guard pushed him farther down the hall, away from her.

He caught her eye. "Everything's going to be all right," his expression said. "I'm here."

Warmth flooded her. *It would be all right. We're together, at least*. Her guard released her hands, and the door closed behind her, the lock sliding into place with a decisive *click*.

After testing the doors and windows—locked and guarded on the outside—she lay back on the small bed, helplessness squeezing her heart and a fiery anger burning alongside it.

What the hell had happened to Charlotte; her student and princess—queen. It was still hard to think of her as queen sometimes. Had she truly betrayed them all? Her—their—friends were dead. *Ystrelle ordered … Mysha and Shepherd were* dead.

Tears dampened the pillow beneath her head as she stared at the gossamer canopy of the four poster bed above her. The memory of the first night they'd finally found Charlotte in Roseharbor Palace flickered across her brain. *"Don't rescue me, Natalie. Leave. Save yourselves,"* Charlotte had said. Perhaps they'd underestimated how much Ystrelle had broken Charlotte's mind. Her ranting and state when she arrived at the Abbey from Roseharbor would certainly support that theory.

Yet, if she truly wanted to help Ystrelle, why help them escape the Abbey? Why alert them to Ystrelle's plans to attack?

Natalie chewed the inside of her cheek viciously. Maybe Ystrelle had broken Charlotte—but sometimes Charlotte, the real Charlotte, had been able to emerge from under the psychological rubble. To warn them to get to safety. To help set up the Center and prepare its defenses. Natalie recalled the faraway, distant look that had so often disturbed her about Charlotte since her release from imprisonment. Perhaps that's when Ystrelle's Charlotte took over.

She heaved a sigh. If this was the case, then poor Charlotte had been dealing with significantly more psychological trauma than any of them suspected. And she'd fought through it. For them.

And now Mysha and Shepherd and Goddess knew how many other Center and Obfuselt defenders were dead.

A great sob escaping, she heaved onto her side, smashed a pillow over her head and let the tears come. This had happened on *her* watch. She should have seen, should have known.

The sound of raised voices reached her ears. Victoria Rayvenwood's voice carried quite well. From the sound of it, Jules was giving as good as he got. Another male voice entered the fray; Jules's father, Natalie presumed. Obviously his parents supported Ystrelle's plans. And they still thought their son would listen to them after years of not seeing him for who he was, let alone listening to him.

Natalie strained to hear the voices, but the walls muffled the most of the words if not the volume and emotion. She tried to pay attention but she was so tired. And the room was freezing; no fire had been lit in the hearth. She only had her traveling clothes. The four poster bed had a sheet, a cotton blanket and a dark blue silk coverlet, intricately embroidered with delicate white flowers. Even burying herself beneath these, Natalie still shivered such that her teeth clacked together.

By dawn, she'd barely slept a wink and then only restlessly. Natalie sat up and got dressed sluggishly, rubbing the nagging ache in her neck and swallowing down the nausea.

Great. A migraine. Just what I need.

She was glad to see Jules and Onlo were no worse for wear when they went down the next morning. She overheard Jules's father thanking the innkeeper as his mother accepted a covered basket from a servant. *Right. Can't have the prisoners eating in the dining room with the other guests.*

By the time they reached Roseharbor, her head screamed in protest at the late fall sunlight and the sounds of the city. She vomited over her horse's shoulder. To her dismay, they rode straight past Roseharbor Palace and to the Roseharbor docks.

Each shriek of the seagulls, the immense stench of fish and stagnant water, and the blinding sunlight coming off the water went into her brain like so many spikes and she lost the contents of her stomach again. She didn't dismount her horse so much as fall over and land on a heap on the ground as her guard failed to catch her. She pressed her cheek to the wooden planks of the dock, it's cool wood soothing her head. *If I could just sleep. Or if Ystrelle's going to kill me, just kill me, I wish she would just do it.*

She could hear Jules arguing that she needed Healing but Ystrelle refused his repeated requests. Natalie huffed out a breath. *Ystrelle needs me subdued. How convenient to have a prisoner whose own body keeps them from being a threat. It saves on effort.*

Large hands yanked her to her feet. She stumbled as they dragged her to a small boat that transported her to a galleon waiting at anchor far off shore. *Well, if the headache doesn't kill me, the motion sickness will.*

Natalie didn't protest as she clambered up the rope ladder to the deck of the ship. Nor did she say a word when someone tied her wrists to the rail on the deck above the sterncastle.

"Natalie are you all right?" Jules's deep voice was the best thing she'd heard in ages. Squinting against the pain in her head, she could see Onlo next to her with Jules on the other side of him.

"I'm upright," she replied, swallowing in a vain attempt to quiet her rebellious stomach. "You?"

"Aside from being tied here and forced to talk to my parents, I've been treated with the utmost courtesy and respect. Which is damned unsettling."

One side of Natalie's mouth drew up. "Onlo, how are you? What did Ystrelle do to you?"

"Mostly use me as leverage against Charlotte," Onlo replied, fury simmering in his voice.

Natalie wished she could tell Jules and Onlo of her speculations regarding Charlotte and her state of mind. But Ystrelle's ever present guards made that impossible.

Taking deep breaths for the pain and nausea, she recalled the pink striations she'd seen in the aftermath of the battle at the Center when Ystrelle held a dagger at his throat. "Your neck."

"I'm upright," he parroted, and she managed a smile before dry heaving over the rail, the action causing her head to split in two.

"Nat, if only I could reach you." Jules's voice seemed to come from far away.

"It's ... okay. Been ... through worse," she gasped, wishing for water. "Besides ... no herbs."

The last time she'd traveled by sea, Charlotte had administered and Activated ginger tea along the way and she'd actually been able to enjoy the trip. But Ystrelle had refused her any sort of treatment.

The galleon lifted anchor and Natalie dug her fingernails into the rail, splinters digging into her skin.

"Where are we going?" Natalie rasped.

"We're heading northwest along the coastline," Onlo answered. "But I do not know any more than that."

Jules scanned the sky. "I honestly thought she was taking us to Roseharbor."

"Maybe we're going to Solerin." Onlo speculated.

"Why—"

"It's time," came Ystrelle's order from behind her.
Time? Time for what?

Natalie raised her eyelids against the blinding pain to see a guard untie Jules and take him away. He shot a desperate glance at her. But she soon followed, as well as Onlo, as guards untied their hands from the rail and led to the main deck. *Great, now if I throw up, I can't even do it over the railing.*

Charlotte appeared from under the forecastle, the distant, detached look on her wan face. She came to a stop in front of her master, eyes downcast. Dread slithered in Natalie's stomach; most of the crew had gathered around them.

At a nod from Ystrelle, Jules's guards brought him in front of Ystrelle to face Charlotte.

"What's going on?" he demanded.

The grin that appeared on Ystrelle's face made Natalie shiver. "Why, your marriage, of course."

Jules's parents took their places on either side of Ystrelle.

"For the final time, I will not marry Charlotte."

Ystrelle arched a delicate eyebrow. The sound of metal against leather sounded behind her and Natalie found herself with a dagger pressed against her throat. Her stomach clenched. *Hell in a kettle. Please no. I can't vomit now, I'll slit my own throat.* She swallowed, feeling the skin of her neck press against the blade. A sting and a warm trickle let her know she'd drawn blood.

Jules caught her eye, all color drained from his face. She blinked at him. *Stay alive, Juliers Rayvenwood.*

He blinked back and his shoulders lifted up and down and the sound of his sigh reached her. To her left, Onlo grunted. Rolling her eyes, she spotted he had a knife at his throat as well.

Helplessness rose up and choked Natalie as much as her own motion sickness.

A grin of satisfaction on her face, Ystrelle began the ceremony. Before Ismereld was out of sight, Queen Charlotte Fairisles and Healer Mage Juliers Rayvenwood were husband and wife.

CHAPTER 25

Her guard tied her back to the railing, and not a moment too soon; Natalie threw up over the side, her retching ending in all-consuming sobs. Jules was married. And they hadn't been able to do a thing to stop it.

Natalie opened her eyes a crack to make sure he was all right. Jules and Charlotte followed Ystrelle into the captain's quarters. *Goddess, hopefully not to consummate the marriage.* She collapsed onto the deck, shoulders screaming as they stretched between her body and her bound wrists. The sobbing and awkward position made additional lances shoot through her head.

A comforting weight descended upon her shoulder. Turning, she spied Onlo's dark head resting on her. She heard him taking deep breaths. They'd both just watched their loved ones marry each other. If anyone knew how she felt right now, it was the man whom she regarded as the big brother she never had. Tilting her head so it rested against his, Natalie took a deep, shuddering breath.

"That's the worst thing Ystrelle has ever done to me," he said, voice trembling.

Natalie took a hiccupping breath. "This might sound strange, but as horrible as that was to witness, considering the state of Charlotte's mind, that might be for the best. I don't know what your death would do to Charlotte."

She felt a warm huff of breath on her back.

"How are we going to get through this, Onlo?"

"I don't know."

She closed her eyes and drew as much comfort from her friend as she could.

It was just past sunset when they arrived in port in West Effrin, Solerin, which Natalie had only seen once before— this past summer, when Jules and Charlotte came for their training. Onlo's speculation was correct. *But why are we here?*

They disembarked and Natalie would've crawled out of her skin for a drink of water or the chance to scratch her raw wrists where she had rope burns. She'd long ago lost feeling in her hands and the cold had taken up permanent residence in her bones. As it was, she found herself forced on another horse behind Onlo and led through the frost-tinged Solerin countryside.

She thought back to the beauty of the farms and gardens this past summer. Jake had been with her then and she'd been so preoccupied thinking that Jules and Charlotte loved each other and she'd never be able to touch Jules again.

Now the landscape was dead; the only sound was the crunch of the horses' hooves on the frosty ground. Though she might find the silent sparkling landscape beautiful on another day, Jules and Charlotte were now married against their will and she was a prisoner.

It was almost sunrise when they arrived at a familiar set of cottages along the shores of Lake Jyrenn. Slumping into the arms of her ever present guard, Natalie's entire body protested having to walk again. She half limped and was half dragged into a cottage. She overheard Ystrelle telling Jules and Charlotte to rest well as she needed them for a very important ritual in the morning. She should probably care about that but her body and mind were too numb; the exhaustion overwhelming. She collapsed on a cot and let the pain and fatigue induced fog roll over her in waves.

She was vaguely aware of the mattress sinking beside her. Dully, she opened her eyes to see Onlo's concerned face peering down at her.

"What does she wint waith-want with-them?" Natalie mumbled through cracked lips.

"I do not know. But we won't be ready for it if you are half dead."

Natalie huffed. "I'm sure Ystrelle will bring me Jules or Charlotte and all the medications I need. She's nice like that." Her tongue felt thick. *This bed is so cozy. I'll just fall asleep now.*

"Nat, I'm serious."

"I'm serious, too, so stop waking me up. I'm a Healer and I can do nothing about this." Her voice raised and all her anger at her weak body—a body that used to be able to spar with Onlo for hours on end—came roiling out with a force that astonished even her. "I can't Heal off of Ismereld. Only Healer Mages can do that and—"

"And there's one right here."

"Jules?" Natalie raised her head, peering around like a small kitten who'd just opened its eyes.

"I'm here with Charlotte, who's guarding me," he warned. Nevertheless, her soul lit up as his hand landed gently on her head and she felt his energy combine with hers. She curled in on herself and bit her knuckle, desperate to reach out to him but scared to do so because his wife—*his wife*—was there and might kill or hurt them both if she tried anything.

"Dehydration, a migraine, inflammation in too many joints to count," he muttered. "Charlotte, I need water, dullanbark and fidelia weed. I'm going to leave and see what I can find, all right?" His voice was careful and measured as if talking to a spooked horse.

"Yes. What is the fidelia weed for?"

Natalie listened to Jules explain the treatment and her heart lurched when he left. Ystrelle must be feeling magnanimous because he returned with all the herbs she needed, plus extra blankets. Charlotte used her magery to light a fire on their hearth.

Burying herself under the warm blankets and enjoying the glow of the fire despite the circumstances, Natalie accepted her cup of medicinal tea from Jules. Desperate to feel relief, she gulped the liquid, scalding her tongue. Once she'd got it all down and inhaled just a bit of fidelia smoke, Jules placed his hand on her again and she felt his energy flow through her, Activating both the dullanbark and fidelia. Her pain lessened, and she felt younger by several years instantly.

"Thank you," she croaked, gazing at him.

He trailed a fingertip from her temple to her chin. "You're welcome," he whispered. His Adam's apple bobbed. "Keep drinking water. Even magic can't fix dehydration." He gazed at her, emerald eyes shining with tears. "I need to go. I will see you in the morning. Take care of yourself."

She reached for him with her bound wrists. "But you—"

"I'm fine, Nat. Rest and get better. Ystrelle says there's to be a big ritual tomorrow so we *all* better be ready." He made sure to catch her eye when he emphasized the word "all."

He and Charlotte left, which set off Natalie's sobs again. She felt like a helpless, stupid crying mess. *How could I possibly help with whatever plan Jules has up his sleeve? Earlier this summer, when I was at the height of my fitness and skills, sure.* Before they'd had to battle Aldworth and Ystrelle and her body had decided to never be the same again.

And even that sacrifice was for nothing. Jules was married, they were never going to be together and Ystrelle would wreak havoc on the Isles—and she could do nothing.

The mattress sank again and Onlo put his bound wrists over her head and pulled her close. "Shh, Nat."

It felt like he should say "it will be all right" next, but he didn't. And she was thankful. Both of them knew it wouldn't be all right. Onlo's own love was caught up in all this as well. He must be as angry and petrified as she. Feeling the fidelia weed start to take effect, along with being warm for the first time in days, she whispered her thanks to Onlo and fell asleep.

CHAPTER 26

At dawn, Natalie reluctantly extricated herself from Onlo. Most of her wanted to just hide in bed, but the strong need to pee proved an excellent motivation.

Natalie figured she must be feeling better because, instead of feeling submissive to her guards, she gave them a derisive snort as if they should know to keep up.

"Keep your bloody distance and look away," she demanded. Behind a tree, she managed to relieve herself with her hands tied. *Well, I'm no longer an expert at the short staff but I can pee with my hands tied. So that's something.*

She dipped her hands in Lake Jyrenn to wash them, and splashed her face, trying to dispel the last of the fog from the trials her body had endured the last two days.

Her hope that there'd be food in the communal cottage proved correct when she found it occupied by Ystrelle, Charlotte and Jules, and Jules's parents. All parties sat at the handmade wooden table, the tension thick enough to cut with a knife.

Ystrelle delicately took a bite of eggs and sipped from a teacup with her long fingers in a perfect arch. She looked quite pleased with herself. Charlotte and Jules kept their eyes on their plates. Jules met her gaze briefly when she came in, but looked away.

Natalie helped herself to as much scrambled eggs and bacon as she thought her stomach could handle, plus a bit of apple preserves.

Sitting down, she decided she'd had enough. Several days of pain and sickness usually made her tetchy and she saw no reason to change that just because she was Ystrelle's prisoner. "So, what's the ritual all about today?"

"Queen Charlotte and her husband are going to remove Jyrenn from the sunstone megalith and return him to his physical form."

Jules choked on his tea. "We don't even have the spells for that."

Ystrelle reached into her fur cloak, retrieved a rectangular brown object and placed it on the table. It was a book, its pages yellowed with ages and brown leather cover so stiff it creaked as she opened it to a specific page. "I took the liberty of looking up the spell in our library."

"Convenient," Jules muttered.

"Necessary," Ystrelle arched an eyebrow. "If I left you to research the spell, I'd be waiting for Jyrenn for months as you dragged things out, plotting with your friends to kill me and escape."

Natalie cocked one eyebrow at her forkful of eggs. *Logical.*

"And I suppose, if Charlotte or I refuse you'll just threaten to kill Onlo and Natalie again."

"Of course."

Simple as that. *Jules must do the spell or I die.* Natalie lost her appetite and set her forkful of eggs down on her plate.

Jules held out his hand. "Show me the spell, please."

As he pulled the tome to him, his eyes flashed to Natalie's, his love for her and desire to keep her safe nearly consuming her on the spot. She lowered her eyes to her plate and played with her food. Despite her earlier bravado, she tried and failed to keep the tears from spilling down her cheeks.

Natalie stood on the gray slate surrounding Solerin's glowing sunstone megalith as Jules and Charlotte prepared for the ritual. She'd listened to Jyrenn's voice here and helped write down his teachings while Charlotte and Jules learned how to control their unruly magery. And she sparred with Onlo until sweat drenched her clothes and her muscles screamed at her. Had it only been this past summer when she'd done these things?

She closed her eyes and remembered the feel of giving herself over to all of Onlo's training, turning off her brain and letting her body instinctively use the staff. It was here she'd finally bested him; and it was a skill that saved her life during their disastrous attempt to infiltrate Roseharbor Palace.

Dammit, I know there was no other choice when we were in that throne room; I had to give that energy to Jules so we could get away. But now we're in trouble and I'm just a useless bystander.

Natalie gasped as her guard, a woman a good foot taller than she was, braced an arm across her chest, pulled Natalie to her and pressed a dagger against her throat.

"Are you stalling, Mage Rayvenwood?" Ystrelle demanded.

Jules held up both hands. "No. The ritual is complicated and needs a lot of preparation. Tell your guard to release Natalie."

"He's telling the truth, my lady." Charlotte added submissively. "In all our training this past summer, we never attempted something like this."

The blade moved away from Natalie's throat and the guard let her go. She took several deep breaths trying to steady herself.

Everyone stood waiting while Jules and Charlotte thumbed through the spell, muttering, practicing and conversing with each other to make sure they had it right. At long last, they drew an intricate symbol on the ground in front of the monolith with charcoal and Charlotte announced: "We're ready."

Natalie fought the urge to rock back and forth shaking her legs, which had fallen asleep from standing so long.

Ystrelle sat on one of the stone chairs built into the wall surrounding the megalith, a wistful look on her face. "Finally, I'll get to hold you my love."

Natalie looked at her askance as Jules and Charlotte started chanting the spell together in a language she didn't recognize. *Just how many times did Ystrelle come out here to listen to Jyrenn? Enough to become fanatically obsessed with him, obviously.*

A deep thrum emanated from the megalith; Natalie raised her bound hands over her head trying to cover her ears. The sound somehow wound its way inside her, threatening to shake her apart.

The hum changed into a dissonant throb that escalated to a high pitched *pop*.

Ears ringing in the silence, Natalie lowered her hands and cracked her eyelids open. Charlotte and Jules bent over, supporting themselves on their thighs, chests heaving.

Jyrenn wasn't there.

Oh sh—

"You did this on purpose," Ystrelle shouted, striding up to Charlotte and slapping her. Charlotte collapsed and didn't move.

A guard seized Natalie from behind, her gasp vibrating on the ice-cold edge of the dagger against her neck. Onlo grunted; she could only assume the same thing had happened to him.

"No," Jules roared.

"YOU DID THE RITUAL IMPROPERLY ON PURPOSE."

"I didn't—we, didn't. We simply weren't saying the

words at the exact same time."

Ystrelle sneered. "A likely excuse. Guard, kill—"

"He's right," a strong, but firm voice came from the ground. Charlotte pushed herself to her feet, her normally poker-straight silver hair hanging in dull gray strands around her face. "He's not lying, don't kill anyone. We need to do it again."

Ystrelle pursed her lips.

Natalie's heart beat a tattoo against her ribs, a faint echo beating against the edge of the blade on her throat.

"Fine. Begin. Fail again and Miss Desmond and Mr. Osei both die."

CHAPTER 27

Jules and Charlotte began chanting again. Natalie smashed her elbows over her ears, cursing the rope that dug into her wrists. Distantly, the mage's chanting increased speed. A blazing beam of light shot skyward from the megalith. Natalie squeezed her eyes shut and screamed as the thrumming reached an unbearable level.

From behind her eyelids, the light dimmed slightly and she squinted. Gold light coalesced in front of the megalith. Jules and Charlotte were on their knees, nearly falling over with the effort of maintaining their chant, hair plastered to their faces with perspiration. A trickle of blood, scarlet against her alabaster skin, ran down Charlotte's upper lip.

The amorphous, luminous form became the shape of a man. First, it was just a vague outline. Then Natalie could make out untidy chin length hair framing a wide, generous face. The light faded into the man and the horrid thrum faded, leaving her skin itching as if a thousand ants crawled beneath it.

There, in front of the stone in which his spirit had lived

for two thousand years, stood Jyrenn. One of the Five Mages in the flesh.

Jyrenn scanned the crowd, silver eyes taking in the sight of everyone staring at him, dumbfounded. Silver locks of hair framed his face, despite his obvious youth. He was tall, almost as tall as Jules, with broad shoulders and he wore simple clothing: a white linen shirt, brown linen pants and leather sandals. His eyes alighted upon Ystrelle.

"It's you," a deep voice said.

Natalie jumped. For some reason, she hadn't expected him to sound exactly like the voice she'd heard over the summer.

Ystrelle rose, trembling. "Yes," she whispered. "You recognize me?"

Jyrenn's smile was wide and honest. "I do. You came to listen to me so many times. Since you were a child."

"As soon as the Secret Keeper before me passed on the knowledge of how to access your teachings, I started sneaking out here just to listen to you." Ystrelle blushed.

"You are the Secret Keeper. But you are not a mage. Why did you listen to my lessons?"

"Because I—I enjoyed listening to you; getting to know you."

"I could hear you speaking back to me. I often wished I could say something in return. I was grateful for the company."

Ystrelle bit her lip, eyelashes fluttering. "I often felt like …"

Jyrenn padded over to her and took her hand. "Like what?"

"Like you somehow understood me. Down to my very soul."

Oh, Goddess. Ystrelle fell in love with a man in a rock. Five—well, minus Jyrenn—help us all if he's in love with her too and they start working together.

"I do. More than you know."

Ystrelle beamed and drew him closer to her, blinking in

disbelief like a child in front of a large, delicious piece of chocolate cake.

"So why all the guards? And are these two all right?" Jyrenn dropped Ystrelle's hand and kneeled to examine Jules.

"They are the mages who got you out; your students from earlier this summer."

"Yes, I see" a line creased Jyrenn's forehead as he placed his hands on Jules. "He's used up all his energy during the ritual. And that is not a ritual for the average mage. Also …" One corner of Jyrenn's mouth turned up. "This man is a descendant of me and my wife."

Natalie's eyes widened. Jules was a descendant of two of the Five Mages? *Ugh, I should have put it together. He and Anli had told her. "Aldworth and his associates wanted to abduct descendants of the mages who created the megaliths on the Isles. We didn't know Jules was one of them,"* Anli had said.

"Apparently I have green eyes for a reason." Jules had added.

Green eyes for the descendant of the mage who created the emerald megalith—Bridhe. And Bridhe was married to Jyrenn.

Jyrenn kneeled next to Charlotte. "This woman has used up her energy as well. And," he tenderly moved a lock of hair from her face. "She is also a descendant of my wife and I."

Natalie stifled a gasp. The familiar silver eyes and hair. Charlotte looked so very much like Jyrenn.

Now, two thousand years later, Jyrenn frowned at his many times great-granddaughter lying unconscious at his feet. His forehead creased and his head cocked to the side, a terrible sadness lacing his voice. "There's something else, though. I'm no Healer like my wife, Bridhe, was, but I do have some Healing skill. Her mind is … broken."

Damn right it is.

"Yes, the poor thing has been suffering so. Can you Heal her?" Ystrelle implored.

Natalie rolled her eyes as Onlo made a strangled growl next to her.

"I think so," Jyrenn placed both hands on Charlotte's head, closed his eyes and concentrated.

Natalie waited with bated breath. Could Jyrenn reverse Charlotte's psychological damage? Such a feat was certainly out of the realm of current Healing knowledge. *It certainly couldn't be done by a living Healer, but one of the Five ...*

After what seemed like an eternity, Jyrenn removed his hands from Charlotte. "She should be better than she was. We'll see how much so when she regains consciousness."

Peering around at the assortment of people surrounding the megalith—Ystrelle, Jules's parents, two unconscious mages, two prisoners and many guards, he lifted an eyebrow and turned to Ystrelle. "Why did you have them remove me from the stone? Is there some sort of emergency?"

"No, I just ... wanted to see you. And I—"

"Why do you have so many guards? Certainly you knew I wouldn't be a danger to you."

Ystrelle's laugh was high and rapid. "Of course, but you know—"

Jyrenn frowned and folded his arms. "I don't know. Please enlighten me."

Panic flashed in Ystrelle's eyes. Unable to hold his gaze, she looked away.

"Did the mages perform this ritual of their own volition? You said you wanted to see me. But you are not a mage and there is no emergent situation. You wanted to *see* me but you don't *need* me."

"I-I do need you."

"And the people whose hands are bound? Why are they here? What have you done, Ystrelle?"

"What I had to do," Ystrelle's voice regained its normal commanding tone, if tinged with desperation. "I got you out."

"By any means necessary?"

Ystrelle didn't reply; she simply glared at him. Jyrenn turned his back to her and walked over to Onlo. Natalie gaped; one of the Five Mages stood right next to her. And he seemed on the verge of putting together who Ystrelle was. *Please help us.*

"The scars on his throat. Why does he have those?"

Ystrelle made a jittery response that Natalie didn't hear because Jyrenn moved in front of her. His gaze pierced hers. "She has a cut on her throat as well." he put his hands on her head. Energy such as she'd never felt before cascaded into her body like the loveliest of waterfalls. "She is recovering from dehydration, a migraine and brain damage."

Jyrenn dropped his hands and strode over to Ystrelle. "I don't know what happened to the girl who used to sneak out and listen to me, but you've changed, Ystrelle. For the worse. You are someone who makes sure she gets what she wants and damn the consequences—even if those consequences are people." He drew himself up to his full height, deep voice echoing throughout the small island. "I do not want anything to do with you."

He turned and walked away.

"No, Jyrenn, please, I'll do anything—"

"I think you've done enough. You said that I spoke to your soul. Hear this, now: my soul is of the light. Yours is steeped in darkness."

A primal scream emerged from Ystrelle and she ran at Jyrenn, arms churning, face ablaze. Jyrenn lifted one hand like it was an afterthought and froze her in place. Everyone, including Ystrelle's mages, stood dumbfounded at this display of power.

Keeping Ystrelle at bay, Jyrenn kneeled down next to Charlotte and placed a hand on her forehead. "Be well my daughter."

He bent next to Jules and rested his hand on Jules's temple. Jyrenn kept his hand on Jules for several minutes, forehead creased and eyes closed. "Remember," he uttered finally.

Standing, he said "Fare well, my children." With a brief glance at Ystrelle, he closed his eyes and began chanting in the same language Jules and Charlotte used to summon him. Limned in a yellow glow, he dematerialized, turned into a small ball of light that shot straight to the center of the sunstone megalith.

CHAPTER 28

Ystrelle collapsed to the ground, released from Jyrenn's spell. She turned over on her back panting, jaw open. Pushing to her feet, she ran to the stone and put a trembling hand on it. "Jyrenn? Jyrenn!" Desperation tinged her voice. She spoke the incantation to begin his mage lessons.

Nothing happened.

Ystrelle repeated the spell twice more. She bent her elegant head and rested it on the sunstone.

For reasons Natalie couldn't fathom, tears poured down her own face. She'd only learned about Jyrenn's existence in the stone over the summer. And now Ystrelle didn't have him. Couldn't get to him. No matter how many times she pounded the rough sunstone. Jyrenn was gone. It made no sense for her soul to ache. No sense at all.

A movement caught her eye; she'd been so distracted by the spectacle that she hadn't noticed Charlotte and Jules regain consciousness and sit up.

But Ystrelle did. She pointed a shaking finger at Charlotte. "This is your fault," she shrieked and ran straight at Onlo. Dragging him in front of Charlotte, Ystrelle drew her jewel encrusted dagger, and pressed it against his throat. Onlo roared as blood poured down his neck.

Ystrelle glared daggers at Charlotte. "I'll kill him for this."

Charlotte held up a hand and shot a well-aimed fireball at Ystrelle's gown, which caught fire. Ystrelle released Onlo, dropped and rolled on the ground.

"You will *not*," Charlotte's voice echoed, thick with emotion but commanding nonetheless.

With their leader on the ground, all hell broke loose. Charlotte rushed to Onlo, and burned his bonds apart. He happily dispatched the nearest guard and took her weapons: two daggers, his favorite.

Jules appeared in front of her, holding her shoulders. "Hold still," his emerald green eyes bored into hers. She heard a small zap and, for the first time in days, she could move her hands. She rubbed her wrists as well as she possibly could around the bloody rope burns.

"We'll Heal those later; I'm going to help Onlo," he drew her in for a kiss that made her weak in her knees before letting her go.

Jules and Onlo launched themselves at the guards. Charlotte turned, hands raised, palms glowing orange to attack Ystrelle. Unfortunately, Ystrelle's guards had formed a wall in front of her while Charlotte freed Onlo.

A grin that made Natalie shiver all the way down to her knees spread across Ystrelle's face. She'd just calculated the odds and they were in her favor. Bolts of ice, balls of fire and electricity and shards of stone flew across the courtyard as Ystrelle's guards, many of whom were mages, attacked Jules, Onlo and Charlotte.

Dropping to the ground out of the line of fire, Natalie crawled across the gray slate out of the conflict. She was not a mage and she wasn't a fighter any longer.

On the other side of the knee high stone wall that surrounded the area, Natalie surveyed the battle helplessly. Her love and two friends stood in the middle of twenty or thirty mages attacking them with everything they had. Natalie had no idea how long they could last. Normally, she'd say a long time, but Jules and Charlotte had just performed a complicated ritual. She had no idea how they felt after Jyrenn's Healing. And Onlo, along with her, had been bound for several days. His muscles must be aching.

A foe landed on the ground in between her and the fight itself. Judging from the blue energy crackling over his clothing, he'd been hit by one of Jules's energy bolts. She spied the short staff on his back. Natalie rubbed her fingers together.

Should I do it?

Could I do it?

What about my friends? If I take this staff and enter this battle, will they be safer or in more danger?

I don't know. But I'll never know for sure unless I grab that staff and get in there.

Natalie bounced on her toes and rolled her shoulders.

But she didn't move anywhere.

Her head spun. Somehow, the fight slowed down. Fireballs arced through the air like shooting stars. The light of the sunstone glinted off the ice and stone shards hurtling through the air. Blue electricity sparked in the background.

Running for the fallen guard, legs moving as if they were mired in mud, she fell beside him. Pushing him over, she heaved the staff from his back and lurched to her feet.

Lungs heaving from the effort, she braced her palms on her knees. *Come on, body, we've got to do something.* She surveyed the battle.

Dammit, I just can't stand here. Even if I hit one person and then get killed, at least I'll die alongside friends. It's probably suicide, but I'm going to help.

Jules had run out of energy to supply his magic and was fighting hand to hand as were most of Ystrelle's mages. Charlotte had found a sword, but Natalie spotted the occasional fireball from her. Onlo fought valiantly but he, too, was fading. Their enemy knew it and the group seemed to close in as one.

A plan popped into Natalie's head and she didn't even pause to debate its soundness. She turned and scurried back over the wall and crawled along the perimeter. When she clambered over the wall she was behind Ystrelle, Jules's parents and their wall of guards.

Crouching low, she tiptoed behind them, hardly believing Ystrelle could be this foolish and praying it wasn't a trap. All her guards faced the battle; she only had guards on either side of her and in front. Her back was completely exposed.

They'll all turn and kill me as soon as I hit her. I wish I had a dagger or sword so that I could kill her from behind. But a staff was all she had. And hopefully that would be enough.

Keeping her eyes on the back of Ystrelle's head, she grasped her staff and started running.

Shouts from her left brought her up short. Natalie stared; she didn't recognize the uniforms, but she sure did recognize the faces. The mages Jules had trained at the Center entered the fray. A barrage of magery flew in the air once again.

Natalie slid and fell on her bottom, mouth agape. Leading the new arrivals was none other than Head Councilwoman Geeta Ramesh.

An eerie silence filled the island as Ystrelle's remaining forces took stock of the new arrivals. Then as one, they charged.

In light armor and armed to the teeth with throwing knives, the Head Councilwoman handily took out anyone who made it past the mages. With renewed vigor, Charlotte, Jules and Onlo took out all foes in their reach.

In a few short moments, all that was left was Victoria and Raymond Rayvenwood, Ystrelle, and two mages on her left and right.

Natalie and Charlotte caught each other's eyes and sprinted toward Ystrelle.

"I've got her," Natalie growled.

"No, she's mine," Charlotte yelled back.

Charlotte held out a hand, reducing Ystrelle's last two guards to ashes. Natalie begged her own body not to fail her as she feinted as if to take out her foe's legs, and then twirled her staff around at the last second to smash Ystrelle across the temple.

Charlotte incinerated her before she fell.

Panting, Natalie eyed the smudge of ash on the ground, threw her arm across Charlotte's shoulders and nodded. "Sharing works, too."

CHAPTER 29

Natalie found herself swept up from behind.

"You were brilliant," Jules said, kissing her thoroughly.

Natalie kissed him back, hands scraping the stubble on his chin. "All I did was hit Ystrelle. You three defeated all these mages."

Jules set her down and wiped a blood-soaked sleeve across his forehead, making him look truly gruesome. "'Didn't do anything', don't think I didn't see you sneaking around to take Ystrelle out from behind."

"A move worthy of someone from Obfuselt," Onlo's merry eyes twinkled and he grasped Charlotte's hand, gazing deeply into her eyes.

Just as their gaze began to make Natalie a little nauseous, Charlotte whirled to face them. "Jules, you know I love you right." It was a statement, not a question.

Jules made an exaggerated bow to her with one leg in front of the other and added a flourish with his hand. "Yes, my queen."

"Oh, shut up. I love you but I'm annulling our marriage as soon as possible."

"Good. I don't want to be married to you, either."

"Children, please?" the Head Councilwoman joined them after having retrieved and cleaned her throwing knives. "We have plenty to take care of. Let's start by cleaning this mess up."

"How did you know where to find us, Head Councilwoman?"

Geeta Ramesh arched a dark eyebrow at Natalie. "If I told you, I wouldn't be as mysterious, would I? I do have a reputation to uphold, Headmistress."

Two of Geeta's lieutenants brought Jules's parents in front of them.

Raymond Rayvenwood's face suffused with red as he struggled to break free and get to them. "You'll regret you ever did this!"

"I wanted to say goodbye to you, my son," Jules's mother somehow managed to look prim and proper even in her bonds.

Jules snorted. "'My son?' Be honest, Mother, I was never your son. Or Father's. Not really. You never loved *me*. You only ever loved what I could do for the family."

"Now Juliers, calm down. That is entirely un—"

"It is true. Every bit. And, in case you haven't noticed, I'm done trying to earn your esteem. I am happy doing what I do and being with the woman I love. If that does not make you happy, then you are no family of mine."

Jules stalked away towards the rowboats. More than ready to go home, Natalie started to follow.

"Stay away from my son, you low-born whore," Victoria Rayvenwood hissed.

Jules turned with a truly frightening expression on his face, but before he could say or do anything, Natalie slapped her. "If you need a Healer for your face, come to the Bridhe Center for Healing and Magical Arts. Your son is one of the best we have."

The guard dragged Jules's mother away. Jules raised his shaking hand to Natalie's cheek. "I'm so sorry. I—she—"

Natalie curled her arms around Jules's shoulders. "I know. I know my wo-own worth. She can't take it from me."

"You're an amazing woman, Natalie Desmond."

She grinned and drew him in for a kiss.

Standing at the bow of the ship bound home for Ismereld, Natalie admired the sun sparkling on the gray waters of Bridhe's Channel. Despite the chilly late fall weather and sea winds, Natalie choose to wrap herself in soft, warm blankets and stood on deck, wind whipping her hair around her face and enjoying the rushing sound of the hull making its way through the water.

Her sea sickness, which her queen was only too happy to treat with warm ginger tea that she Activated herself, stayed at bay. Although she sometimes envied Jules and Charlotte their mage-given ability to Heal on any Isle, Natalie did not miss spending sea voyages vomiting over the railing.

Under all her blankets, her fingers curled around the smooth, warm wood of the short staff she'd kept after yesterday's battle. It reminded her of the staff she'd found in the snowy forest the day she decided to accept the position of Headmistress.

I can't train with the staff anymore. But I still helped during the fighting. All I had to do was stay out of the battle until I saw my opportunity—and took it.

Perhaps I was wrong. Although I can't do many of the things I used to, my body is still capable. As long as I am mindful of when and how I use my energy, I can still be productive. I can be the Headmistress and Healer people need.

A flash of white and gray caught Natalie's eye. Grasping the salty, damp railing, she bent toward the water. Several large gray streaks sped just beneath the waters' surface. Three of them got closer to her and then arced gracefully out of the water at the same time.

"Dolphins," Natalie squealed.

169

The sailors grinned at her and then went about their work. Jules took the stairs up to the forecastle two at a time and peered over the railing next to her.

Weaving deftly in an out of the water, the dolphins played with each other and the ship, merrily splashing in and out of the water.

Natalie shuffled sideways so her shoulder touched Jules's. Meeting his gaze, they beamed at each other. The sea air pulled at Jules's short, dark hair and sprinkled it liberally with salt. His cheeks and ears reddened from the cold. The sun sparkled in his emerald green eyes. Helpless, she stood unmoving.

"Nat."

"Yes?"

"I—I don't—I didn't grow up with the best example of a family. At home, at any rate. My family was always the Abbey," he pulled his eyes from hers and stared out at the horizon.

Natalie rested her head on his shoulder.

"So I likely have a lot to learn. With that being said," Jules turned to her and fished her hand out from under her blankets. "Will you do me the honor of being—"

Natalie launched herself into his arms. "Yes!"

Jules caught her, overbalanced and they toppled onto a pile of coiled lines. Natalie shrieked and Jules's breath came out in a muffled *oof!*

"—my wife," he groaned.

Natalie dipped her lips to his, slipping her hands out of the blanket and twining them around her fiancée.

"Yes," she whispered.

"I love you," he breathed before kissing her back.

CHAPTER 30

Charlotte annulled the marriage between herself and Jules the day they returned to Roseharbor.

She immediately began setting to rights the damage done by her parents, Aldworth and Ystrelle.

One of the first orders of business was freeing all the captive family members of mages. Natalie and Jules helped Charlotte organize Healing for any privations they suffered. Treating the men, women and children on the verge of starvation made her want to kill Ystrelle all over again.

The grief of the families whose mages died in the attack on the Center or at the sunstone megalith sent Natalie pacing restlessly around the palace at night.

Charlotte and Geeta were thick as thieves planning how the country would work from now on with the monarchy and the Council of Isles working hand in hand.

Natalie and Jules had their own meeting with the Head Councilwoman before their departure for the Center.

"I thank you for your invitation when we first met, but I'm not ready to be on the Council of Healers," Natalie stated, wrapping her fingers around a mug of warm spiced apple cider. "Being Headmistress is more than enough for me, at least for now. In fact, with the Council's permission, I'd like to take on an assistant when I return to the Center."

The Head Councilwoman nodded. "Whatever you need to make it work. I'm sure it hasn't been easy balancing self-care and your Headmistress duties."

"Oh, there's been no balance whatsoever," Natalie said cheerfully. "My body needs extra help. I must stop overexerting myself in an attempt to prove to everyone that I can be Headmistress. After everything that's happened the past few days, I finally realized that it doesn't matter how Headmistress Gayla did her job or how other people think I should do my job. It matters that I am healthy and do my job well."

Jules squeezed her hand under the table. "I'm willing to join both the Council of Mages and the Council of Healers."

"You've earned it. Let's begin, shall we?"

While Jules and the Head Councilwoman discussed matters of government, Natalie found her way to the queen's suite of rooms. As they sat on cozy chairs next to a crackling fire Natalie glanced over her the steaming rim of her tea cup at the young woman who was her friend, former student, and queen.

"How are you Charlotte? Really?"

"Ystrelle is out of my head. I'm just really sorry that I—"

Natalie held up a hand. "It wasn't your fault."

"Sometimes I understand that. Other times, I think: '*Mysha and Shepherd Harris are* dead. *Little Emma is an orphan and it's all my fault.*'"

Charlotte released the perfect posture she'd maintained since returning to Roseharbor Palace and let her face fall into her palms.

A hundred replies vied to get out of Natalie's mouth. She

was a Healer; she liked to fix things. But maybe this wound was too fresh. "Did Jyrenn fix your mind somehow?" she asked instead.

Charlotte dragged her head from her hands. "Yes. I don't remember anything about it; I wish I did. But yes, he fixed the direct trauma caused by ... by seeing ... by Ystrelle. Now all that's left are the scars caused by the memories of what I did."

"Do you want to talk about it?"

"No," Charlotte whispered.

Natalie fought every Healing instinct she had so she didn't badger Charlotte into talking. *Her problems are like an infection; she must get it out or they will just get worse.*

But Charlotte had also been through more than most in her lifetime. "Promise me you'll talk to someone someday."

"I will."

Natalie twirled her braid and stared into the fire. As the often did of late, memories of Jyrenn's visit nagged her.

"Out with it, Nat. I can hear you thinking from here."

Natalie jumped. "Well, I feel sort of selfish saying this, but Jyrenn fixed a lot of your mind. I'm pretty sure he also Healed Jules's mind. He's had maybe one nightmare since Jyrenn laid hands on him. And what I wonder is ... why didn't he Heal me, too? He even turned to Ystrelle and told her what was wrong with me."

Charlotte shook her head sadly. "He didn't Heal Onlo's throat, either. Seeing those scars every day is ..." Charlotte inhaled sharply and released her breath.

Natalie gave her braid a brutal twist. *I didn't even think of him Healing Onlo.* She took a deep breath and closed her eyes. *Just a reminder that not everything begins and ends with my injury.*

Charlotte interlaced her fingers and rested her chin on them. "I don't know. I wish I did. I wish I could've seen Jyrenn to begin with, but I was unconscious the whole time he was out of the megalith. Judging from what others told me, things deteriorated pretty rapidly between him and Ystrelle when he pieced together what she'd done."

"That's true," Natalie admitted. "But he also held her in place with some sort of spell I've never seen before." Guilt churned in her stomach. Jyrenn had done so much to help them that day. She sounded like a child begging her mother for another piece of candy and crying when she didn't get it.

"Maybe there are things even one of the Five Mages can't fix. Maybe he knew we have the capability of helping you ourselves. Or that you have the ability to Heal yourself."

Natalie snorted. "I think I would have done that by now."

"Maybe you have the ability, but you don't know how to do it yet. Like learning the short staff. You had the ability all along but only recently had the need to learn how to use it."

Natalie chewed her lip thoughtfully. "You're talking about researching my own cure."

"Or at least a way to have a better quality of life even if you can't find a cure."

"Humph," Natalie breathed out, setting her empty cup of tea down in its saucer on the ornately carved wooden table next to her chair.

Natalie stared at the fire again, her troubled thoughts churning through a myriad of subjects, eventually landing on something she'd filed away and sternly reminded herself to tell Charlotte before she and Jules left for home.

"Look," Natalie said. "I don't know if your parents or tutors taught you anything about sex and getting pregnant."

Charlotte's tea cup rattled. "Oh my Goddess, Nat," she choked on her tea, face turning an alarming shade of red. Whether it was from swallowing the tea improperly or the topic, Natalie didn't know.

"Well, you may have fooled a lot of people at court with the tall, dark, handsome new captain of your personal guard. But not me. I see how you and Onlo look at each other. He's ten years older than you are Charlotte. Are you sure—"

Charlotte rubbed the bridge of her nose. "Well, this is a

good beginning. I'm sure people whispering at court will be nothing compared to you just assuming we're having sex."

"I'm not assuming anything, but you're sixteen and I want to be sure you're properly educated. I know you know about moon bark extract, but—"

"Nat! We're not having sex."

Natalie's eyes widened. "You're not? But the way you look at each other ..."

Charlotte held her gaze. "We love each other very much, it's true. But he's well aware that I have a kingdom to run. And I'm well aware that he's much older and still grieving his wife. So yes, we look at each other a lot and sometimes hold each other, but ... we need time."

Natalie's heart ached for her friend. She knew what it was like to love someone from afar and think you could never have them. She thanked the Goddess that, after everything, Jules was hers and she his.

"And what are you going to do if you decide to marry your guard and not make a political alliance?"

"I don't know," Charlotte took another sip of tea and stared into the fire. "Maybe I'll think of something by then."

CHAPTER 31

Riding through the gates of the Center, Natalie couldn't keep a huge grin off her face when she greeted the guards by name.

Her jaw fell open as she and Jules rode toward the main building. *So many changes and improvements since we've been gone; it looks like a proper school and Healing facility now.*

The old barn no longer had a hole in the roof though black clad workers crawled atop the structure still affecting repairs.

Natalie grasped Jules's hand after they'd groomed their horses and they strolled toward the front door. Squinting in the bright sunlight, Natalie nearly jumped out of her boots when a human blur with a white cloth on top flew at her.

"Ohmigoddess, you're alive," Em shrieked, grabbing her tight and spinning her in a circle.

Nat hugged her best friend and laughed. "I know, I can't believe it either,"

In the distance, joyful barks echoed across the grounds and a streak of brown fur shot out of the tall grasses near the lake, hurtling towards Natalie.

"Jake!"

Jake ran and leaped onto her, knocking her to the ground and getting his muddy paws all over the gorgeous clothing Charlotte had given her. She didn't care in the least. But she did care about breathing, which was hard to do with a dog standing on her chest and licking her face.

Hugging Jake, she sat up and told him to sit, which he barely managed given his wagging tail made his butt shake so hard.

"Anli," Jules greeted, shaking Anli's hand. "Glad to see your recovery continues to go well."

Natalie grinned at her friends from behind a face full of dog. "I take it our plan to have you two run the Center in case something happened to me worked?"

Em grinned and squeezed Anli's hand. "It did."

Natalie spied the baby on Anli's hip. "Thank you for taking care of everyone and everything while we were gone. Is that baby Emma?"

"It is," Anli said in a sing-song voice.

Anli has a sing-song voice?

"We're awaiting permission from Obfuselt to adopt her. We're getting married."

"Ohmigoddess," it was Natalie's turn to shriek and she scrambled to her feet, hugging Em.

"Don't even think about it, Headmistress," Anli said when Natalie would have hugged her as well.

Natalie grasped Em's hand and walked toward the Center door. "Tell me about after the battle." Her voice was thick with grief for Mysha and Shepherd.

Em squeezed her hand. "We buried the Ismereld bodies behind the Center. Amongst all the things we needed as a Center for Healing, a graveyard unfortunately moved to top priority after the battle. We buried the bodies on the mountain side far from our water sources."

"The Obfuselt bodies we buried at sea. It was…" Anli's voice faded.

"It was sunset. The Priestess said a prayer asking the sea to return them to the Goddess. It was beautiful, really," Em rubbed her palm across her cheek.

Sobs rose in Natalie's chest and threatened to choke her. There'd been a lot of deaths during her first few months of being Headmistress. Hopefully, with Charlotte restored to the throne and Ystrelle and Aldworth off the table, she could return to saving lives.

"I want to see the graveyard. And where the burial at sea was."

"You will," Jules clasped her other hand. "Let's go home first.

Entering the door of the Center, students and staff alike swarmed Natalie and Jules, wanting to know about their time in Ystrelle's clutches and if she was dead.

Natalie held up a hand. "Let us get food and we can tell the whole story over dinner."

An amazing number of people crammed into the new dining hall, plates full of luscious cuts of beef, buttery mashed potatoes and pear preserves, courtesy of the local farmers who were all too eager to support Ismereld's Healing flagship in their community.

Food getting cold, Natalie and Jules sipped ale and told the Center all about their abduction, what happened at the Solerin megalith, and the restoration of the queen's mind.

Both Natalie and Jules emphasized that after Jyrenn had Healed her; Charlotte was no longer the person controlled by Ystrelle, the person who betrayed them.

"I think he did something to me, too," Jules whispered once their audience moved on to finishing their food and discussing the story animatedly amongst themselves. No doubt the story had changed several times already.

"I know," Natalie whispered back. "You're having fewer nightmares than you did before." Natalie carefully avoided his eyes so he wouldn't see any lingering resentment toward Jyrenn for not Healing her as well.

"It's more than that. I know more about magic than I

did before."

"Before he went back into the megalith, he put his hand on your head and said 'Remember'. Do you suppose he did something then?" Natalie asked.

Jules arched a dark brow. "Perhaps. I wonder if he conveyed some of his preserved knowledge to me. There is no longer a Secret Keeper on Solerin after all. Unless Ystrelle was training someone, no one knows the spell to start the magery lessons."

Natalie hummed. "The spell to start the lessons no longer works, anyway. And I doubt Ystrelle would share her access to Jyrenn with a Secret Keeper trainee unless it suited her own ends. You and Charlotte learning from him definitely suited her own ends just fine. She wanted the mages to come back and rule."

"Oh, mages are back, but I have no interest in ruling anyone. I see no reason that a mage should have any more social clout than a Healer, a Blacksmith, Dancer, or an apple farmer's daughter."

"I agree, I just wish …" Natalie hesitated, turning her empty ale mug in circles on the table.

"Wish what?"

I might as well tell him. He has to be wondering the same thing. "I wish he'd Healed me and Onlo like he Healed you and Charlotte. I wish Ystrelle hadn't chased him back into hiding before he had the chance."

Jules squeezed her hand.

"We'll keep trying. In the meantime, you can use the fidelia in the evenings again."

After dinner, they ascended the stairway and Natalie opened the door to their suite. It smelled crisp, clean and lovely. Someone had decorated the room with cinnamon and clove scented pine cones in small baskets and bowls. Lorelannish carpets now covered the floor and a tall mahogany four poster bed occupied one side of the room. A gauzy fabric draped over the top and Natalie couldn't wait to see it wafting in spring breezes.

The other side of their suite had three burgundy poufy couches. Books from Gayla's office lined the shining white book shelves surrounding the fireplace.

Spinning about the room, it was hard to care about politics or the state of the Isles. She was *home*. With her *fiancée*.

Beholding her expression, Jules strode toward her and ran his fingers over her cheek and tangled them in her hair. His other arm drew her close, safe with him.

"I'm glad you are mine," Natalie's lips brushed his.

"I am yours," Jules's voice was deep, seductive. "And I'm glad you are mine." He captured her lips with his. Chills skittered down her spine and warmth pooled in Natalie's belly as she lost herself in the kiss. All she wanted was him. Forever.

Jules pulled away from her, touching his forehead to hers. "Marry me."

"I already said yes, you insufferable man." Natalie giggled and kissed his nose. "Will you marry me?"

Natalie's heart nearly burst at the love she beheld in Jules's hooded emerald eyes.

He slowly nodded. "Yes, you insufferable woman. I'm going to kiss you now. And I don't think I'll stop anytime soon."

She ran her palms down the planes of his back. "Excellent plan, Healer Mage Rayvenwood."

CHAPTER 32

Natalie walked down the aisle of Saltwick's Temple of the Goddess in silk slippers and the most exquisite dress she'd ever worn. Designed just for her by Priscilla Rayvenwood, Jules's sister, the plum-colored silk bodice wrapped around her creating a V-neck. The material gathered at the waist and then flowed behind her onto the floor. She beamed at Jules who stood next to Onlo and the queen at the end of the aisle.

Reaching Jules, she threw protocol and ceremony into the wind and kissed him out of pure joy. Turning her expectant gaze to the front of the Temple, she bit her lip and quickly released it when she remembered how long the lady's maid spent applying make up to her face. She prayed she didn't have lip color on her teeth.

The musicians played an ethereal piece that cast a spell over everyone. Pine boughs and wreaths of evergreen branches, holly and pine cones covered the stone walls, echoing the winter solstice landscape outside.

Natalie and the congregation sighed as Em and Anli

entered the building. They both wore Pricilla Rayvenwood creations as well: Em a flowing, elegant emerald green dress with a matching scirpa and Anli form fitting black silk. They carried baby Emma between them, her eyes wide over her round apple cheeks. The baby wore a tiny dress with a simple emerald top and a black skirt with matching lace that puffed out around her chubby legs. With the crown of white snowdrops woven into a wreath atop her ink-black curls, Natalie thought she might die from the cuteness.

The threesome made their way down the aisle to the priestess. Natalie's cheeks ached from smiling so much. By the end of the ceremony, she ended up destroying her make up anyway by sobbing when Em and Anli kissed and the threesome became a family.

The roar of approval from the crowd startled Little Emma and she burst into tears, her face beet red as her mothers held hands and nearly ran back down the aisle, faces radiant. A hand pulled on her shoulder. She turned and looked up at Jules, who had tears of joy dotting his face as well.

"Your face is a mess," he said, dabbing her cheeks with his handkerchief.

"I love you, too." Natalie snatched the cloth from him and dabbed his cheeks and happily succumbed as he slid his hand onto her hip and pulled her in for a long, sensuous kiss.

"Enough you two. There are certain things prohibited in the Temple of the Goddess, you know."

Grinning at her queen, Natalie took Jules's hand. "Then let's go to the feast, shall we?"

Natalie peered into the mirror hanging in the room in which she grew up and adjusted her necklace one last time. The necklace in question, a string of pearls from the oysters in Bridhe's Channel, had belonged to her grandmother, Da's mother.

"You look perfect, of course, silly. How could you not in my dress?" Priscilla Rayvenwood stepped forward and tugged and fussed with a few bits of her dress, fixing imperfections Natalie couldn't see.

"Mother?"

Anna Desmond's eyes shone with tears. "You look lovely, sweeting."

With one last look in the mirror, Natalie made sure everything was just right. Warm spring air drifted in the windows making her emerald green gown sway gracefully, but, thanks to Pris's efforts, the hair piled on top of her head adorned with tiny flowers didn't budge one bit. "Let's go; I don't want to keep him waiting."

Carefully treading down the stairs, lifting her gown and figuring any moment she'd trip and fall, Natalie made her way to the kitchen of her family's home. Memories of thousands of meals shared together swirled in her mind; certainly Da was here with them today.

Aaron, dressed in his apprentice blacks lifted his arm, which she grasped like a lifeline. *Goddess, has he gotten even taller?*

With her family at her side, she walked out into the apple orchard where a small gathering of her and Jules's closest friends sat, the late afternoon sun slanting through the trees. The instant she glimpsed Jules, standing among the blossoming trees, her eyes locked onto his. His gaze consumed her and it was all she could do to stay with Aaron and not run into his arms. Bursting with the wish for time to speed up, it disobeyed her and slowed down as she marched below the apple boughs. The occasional petal fell as if in blessing and the sweet powdery scent of crushed apple blossoms under her bare feet reminded her of the springs of her childhood.

At last arriving in front of the priestess, Aaron passed her hand to Jules's and she grasped it, beaming. *We made it. We're here. Our path here hasn't exactly been an ordinary one. I've no doubt we'll live an extraordinary life together.*

The sun burnished Jules's dark wavy hair. A white apple blossom landed on the fitted black shirt he wore. His emerald green cloak, which matched his eyes perfectly, billowed ever so slightly in the wind and the ends flirted with the polished knee-high boots he wore. He smelled of leather, soap and fresh morning grass, and Natalie stared shamelessly at him like a lovesick schoolgirl, in complete disbelief that he was finally hers.

Jules squeezed her hand and smirked at her. Heat suffused her cheeks as a wave of laughter rippled through the congregation. *Oh, right. Vows.* "We are now one. Juliers Rayvenwood, I vow to be your friend, partner, comfort and haven. From this day forward, we will build a home together filled with love, laughter, joy, and light, no matter what strife comes our way." She swallowed. They'd had their fill of strife, surely. "This I swear from today until I return to the Goddess."

Jules squeezed her hand and his deep voice filled the grove. "We are now one, Natalie Desmond, I vow to be your partner comfort, and haven. From this day forward, we will build a home together filled with love, laughter, joy, and light, no matter what strife comes our way." He winked and a giggle escaped Natalie despite her determination to be solemn. "This I swear from today until I return to the Goddess."

The priestess raised her hands. "May the love of all of us support you in your life together. By the blessings of the Goddess invoked here today, I now declare you man and wife. You may now—"

Natalie grabbed the crisp lapels of Jules's jacket and drew his lips to hers, kissing him deeply before the priestess could finish. Their family and friends roared with laughter.

Jules broke the kiss first. Turning, his hand clasped tightly in hers, they walked back down the blossom-covered aisle. Their friends went by in a blur and Natalie tried to wave and say something to everyone. Anli and Em with little Emma standing, grasping Em's dress with a drool covered fist in her mouth. Charlotte with the white diamond circlet in her hair, resplendent in white with Onlo in his dress blacks next to her. Her mother, holding Jake whose tongue hung out in a big dog grin as his tail beat a steady rhythm on the ground. Aaron in his Obfuselt trainee outfit.

Joy and love filled her heart to bursting and her lip quivered. *Ridiculous. It's my wedding day, I shouldn't cry.*

People whisked the chairs away and the musicians slipped easily from the elegant music they'd played for the ceremony to rollicking jigs and reels. Everyone swarmed the tables laden with fresh roasted meats, root vegetables, fresh baked bread and kegs of beer. Sometime later, plates abandoned, Jules tugged Natalie into the center of the dancers. Whoops and hollers went up and Natalie spun, stepped and swirled with her husband, until breathless, mouths burning with thirst. They both staggered hand in hand to a keg and sipped cold beer.

"Come with me," Jules said huskily, tugging her hand.

Natalie shrieked, reaching to put her cup on the table and praying it stayed and followed her husband into the now dark shadows of the orchard.

He led her behind a particularly large tree and, leaning against the trunk pulled her against him, demanding attentions she was only too happy to give.

Lips swollen and cheeks warm, Natalie pulled away from her husband and bent her forehead to his.

"I love you," he whispered. "I'm so glad I'm spending my life with you."

"I love you, too. Our life so far has been a bit ... turbulent," Natalie observed with a wry grin.

"Most likely it will always be so. But there will always be the two of us."

"Yes. Always."

EPILOGUE

Seven Years Later

Stepping through the balcony doors in the twilight, Natalie let the warmth of the summer night enfold her. Frogs and insects chirped by the lake. A faint breeze cooled her skin while bats swooped overhead in search of an evening meal.

Jake slowly pushed up from his cushion near the doors and limped out to join her. Natalie squatted and stroked his gray muzzle. "Aw, Jake, old buddy. You didn't have to get up if it hurts."

Jake's tail swished the air. He gave her one lick and walked over to the old blanket she kept folded on the balcony just for him. He pawed at it, turned in three circles and laid down with his muzzle resting on his front paws.

"What did you think of your first Council meeting, Councilwoman?"

"Boring," Natalie pronounced.

Jules's laughter echoed off the mountains as he came up behind her and enfolded her in his arms.

"They are that," he agreed.

"It was nice to see Charlotte and Onlo, though."

"It was. And I must say I'm grateful to you. After seven years of serving on both the Council of Healers and the Council of Mages, I am more than happy for you to take my place with the Healers. There is only so much politics a man can take."

Natalie blew her hair out of her face. "Me, too."

Jules smoothed the errant piece of hair down. "How's your head?"

"All right. As long as I keep up with the fidelia, the headaches aren't as severe or as frequent. I'm going to keep researching, though." In Natalie's precious moments of spare time, she holed up in the library researching head injuries, headaches and fatigue. A few times, she'd hit upon potential solutions. Some even worked—for a little while.

"You should. Perhaps there's an answer out there somewhere."

Natalie swallowed, eyes stinging as tears threatened. "Do you think there's an answer for why I can't get pregnant?"

Jules kissed her temple and swayed her back and forth. "Maybe. Em has done so much to help us. I'm sure she'll let us know if she discovers something."

"I just don't understand," Natalie's voice caught. "Women get pregnant all the time. Often without meaning to. Why can't I?"

"It's not your fault, Nat. It takes two to make a child after all. It's possible I can't father children."

"Other mages are now fathers."

"Plenty of couples can't conceive children regardless of magical ability."

Natalie conceded this point, nodding silently with tears streaming down her face.

"We can always adopt like Em and Anli."

Natalie smiled at the memory of little Emma's dark hair shining in the sunlight as she ran up to Natalie proudly showing off her newest lost tooth. "We could."

"At the same time, one could argue that we have about one hundred fifty or so children in this Center. We love them, care for them and support their goals. So far, we're doing better than my parents ever did."

"Well, that's a rather low standard," Natalie said wryly. Jules did have it right though. She loved each and every student here down to the last tearful bad-breakup and sullen silence. Still. "I just always imagined having a family like Mother and Da. Giving a child the same love they gave me."

"I did, too. It was you and your family who first showed me what a family could really be."

Natalie took a shuddering breath. "I don't know. I don't know what the right answer is." Chimes danced across the lake indicating the hour. Even after several years, Natalie still found the sound entrancing.

"Are you happy, Jules?"

"Hmm, let me think now ..."

Natalie reached around and poked his stomach. "Ha ha. I can make you unhappy, you know."

Jules kissed the back of her head. "Well, let's see. I'm still a Healer. I lead mage classes here at the Center and I'm the Head Councilman for the Council of Mages. The number of people trying to kidnap and torture me is down to zero. Oh, and I can't forget my lovely wife."

Natalie turned in his arms and stuck her tongue out at him.

Jules kissed her forehead. "Yes, I'm very happy. What about you?"

Natalie leaned her head back against Jules's shoulder and squeezed his hand with hers.

Am I happy?

Running the Center well, getting through each day with everyone still alive and intact, took up most of her time. Even with the capable assistance of Healer Bishop, her Headmistress duties, often left her with little or no spare time. Watching out for her own health consumed the rest of her day.

Her two-year quest to get pregnant mired her in hopelessness and despair often; she was lucky she had Jules and Em to help her cope.

Still, being Headmistress brought her fulfillment she'd never expected when she took on the job. Seeing struggling children learn to grow and thrive. Watching her students go out into the world and succeed. And, of course, spending time with her loving husband at the end of the day.

Natalie gazed into Jules's emerald green eyes. "Yes. I *am* happy."

THE END

AUTHOR'S NOTE

Natalie spends much of this book adjusting to her new life as someone with a traumatic brain injury (TBI). Although she sustained her TBI from magic, the symptoms and experiences she has as a result are very much grounded in reality.

One of the most obvious was her aphasia. Aphasia.org defines this condition as "an acquired communication disorder that impairs a person's ability to process language, but does not affect intelligence. Aphasia impairs the ability to speak and understand others."

I have aphasia from chronic migraine. My migraines started in my mid-30's. In the beginning, I got about two or three migraines a month. I managed these with yoga, meditation, diet and supplements.

In January 2019, I had sixteen migraine days. Now that's a number that will change your life a wee bit, much like Natalie's. Yoga and meditation now support a rather impressive regimen of anti-seizure medication, Botox®, nerve blocks, and Aimovig™ one of the new medications recently approved by the FDA.

Many of my experiences as a migraineur became Natalie's experiences in *Obsidian's Legacy*. Of course, I didn't include all my experiences, and Natalie's experiences are not all-inclusive of someone with TBI.

The stigma, as Natalie discovered, is real. It can be hard, when a health challenge arises in adulthood, for people to reconcile a person's old capabilities with their new capabilities.

Used as a running gag in this book, the "have you tried …" phenomenon ranges from uncomfortable to annoying. I included some of the more bizarre examples in this novel. Yes, I have actually seen the lemon-on-the-forehead suggestion as well as eating a potato whole. I've also had people tell me that everything will get better with menopause or pregnancy.

I strive every day to remind myself of Natalie's own discoveries in this story: that her illness doesn't define her worth, that she can still contribute and be great at her job, and the past and/or people who don't understand her illness don't define her.

For everyone struggling with health challenges, this is for you. I see you; you are not alone.

If you enjoyed *Obsidian's Legacy*, please leave a review. Even a sentence or two is a big help. Thank you!

Please join my mailing list via katekennelly.com!

All subscribers receive a prequel short story **for free!** As part of my email community, you'll be the first to know about new releases and cover reveals as well as opportunities to receive ARCs and be a beta-reader. You'll also get other good stuff including deleted scenes, alternative POV chapters, short stories, and more.

Please join me on the Internet:
Web: http://www.katekennelly.com
Instagram: @authorkatekennelly
Twitter: @katemkennelly
Facebook: @katemkennelly

ACKNOWLEDGEMENTS

To you, my readers: thank you for reading!

To my beta readers: Angie, Ness and Sue: Thank you for making my story so much better!

A huge shout out to all my cheerleaders who supported and believed in me from the beginning. Your confidence in me mean more than you know.

To Carbon Leaf with gratitude for the decades of music they've given us. Lake Clanairys, and the old hotel that became The Bridhe Center for Healing and Magical Arts, is an homage to their song *Lake of Silver Bells*. Your music means the world to me.

A huge thank you to all the people who let me cast their horses, dogs and cats as characters in this trilogy. I hope I did them justice.

To every single member of my family who is there when I need you. Who stands beside me no matter what. You have my eternal gratitude.

ALSO BY KATE KENNELLY

ISLES OF STONE TRILOGY

Emerald's Fracture

Sunstone's Secret

Obsidian's Legacy

ABOUT THE AUTHOR

KATE KENNELLY started writing creatively when she was ten years old. She let a bad grade on a creative writing project in seventh grade get her down and stopped writing altogether. Many years later, now suffering from chronic pain, someone asked her "When are you not in pain?" The answer was "When I do creative things." Kate challenged herself to sit down and write something–anything–for the therapeutic value. Thirteen chapters later, not only was she writing, but she was reading books on writing, watching YouTube videos, learning all she could to try to craft a good story.

In her free time, Kate loves to play fiddle, do yoga, meditate and play World of Warcraft with her book club friends. She lives in Maryland with her husband, two daughters and two rescue dogs.

Made in the USA
Middletown, DE
24 March 2019